His Dark Sun

Published 2018 by Moth Publishing, an imprint of Mayfly Press

Paperback ISBN 9781911356097

Ebook ISBN 9781911356103

A CIP catalogue record for this book is available from the British Library.

Cover design by courage, UK.

Printed and Bound by cpi colour

Mayfly Press
New Writing North, 3 Ellison Terrace, Ellison Place, University of Northumbria, Newcastle upon Tyne NE1 8ST
www.mayfly.press

His Dark Sun

Jude Brown

MOTH
PUBLISHING

For Audrey.

Thursday, 26th May 2022

The apples sit on the windowsill in the back room. I usually see to them early morning, but reception's been mental, phone's never stopped. It's always this way when Kojak's not around. I'm thinking today might be their last. They've nothing left to offer anymore, juices are well gone. I pick one up. It's all shrunken, wizened, like the rest.

I rotate each apple and when I'm done I look up, catch sight of Malik out the window. He's supposed to be working on the estate. The car needs an MOT and a service, but he's too busy jawing on his mobile. There are three more booked in for the same and it'll be me gets it in the neck if we don't finish on time. I swear at him under my breath and he turns, looks right at me as if he's heard me.

I slope off to Kojak's office. He's not due back until after lunch and he's got one of those big maps on his wall. It'll be easier to check out a route. I know where Leyton is and I know where the site is, but I went in Kojak's car last time. This time I'll be making my way there, and for partway it'll be on foot.

The map isn't that old but it's already outdated.The local streets and neighbourhoods haven't changed, but some of the landmarks are gone. I trace my finger along the river, past the Docklands, Westminster, Kew Bridge. They don't exist anymore, all swallowed up by the big fat Thames. *Like maggot crawling through rotten apple.* That's what Kojak called it. *This city, stinking cesspit. You know problem? Too many bloody foreigners.*

I remember waiting for him to crack a smile, say he was joking, and when he didn't I muttered something about the sewers not being able to cope because they weren't built for this kind of weather. He just slapped me on the back, told me to start Monday.

'So, this is where you're hiding?'

Malik's in the doorway stripped to his waist, his overalls bunched around his hips. He's holding a carton of ice-cold milk and pinpricks of condensation are already forming. The carton glistens like his skin. I step away from the outdated map in its outdated frame, and my foot catches the waste bin beside Kojak's desk. The bin rocks and I will it not to tip over, will it not to spill its contents all over the floor. It spares me, stays upright.

Malik reaches up and thumps the air con unit above the door. It goes from making a low hum to a loud rattle. He takes another swig of his milk and a thin white worm clings to his top lip.

'You need to tell Fat Boy to get some decent shit, not this second-hand crap. The one in the workshop's as bad. Shouldn't have to work in these conditions.'

The milk worm wriggles as he talks. Makes him look even more of a dick than he already is. He drains the carton, punches it into a ball and chucks it at the bin. He misses and makes no move to pick it up.

'You finished the estate?' I say.

He wipes his mouth and the worm disappears. 'We're entitled to regular breaks. It's the law, in case you'd forgotten.'

'Mo seems to cope,' I say.

A *fuck-you* curl of a smile forms on his face.

'That's because he's like you.' He walks towards me, puts his face right in mine. 'A freak.'

He exaggerates the 'k' sound and it echoes inside my head. I tell him he should get back to work. He's six foot two. I'm six foot three. That inch counts.

The front door jangles and I go back to reception. Mrs Goldman's there with Charlie, her chihuahua. She's got him tucked under her arm and he's panting like he's on his last few breaths. She pops him down on the counter, takes out a small bowl and a bottle of water from her handbag and pours him a drink. He laps so hard with his tiny pink tongue that the bowl shuffles along the counter towards me.

'What can we do for you today?' I say, pushing the bowl back to Charlie.

2

'Full service, please, soon as you can. We're off up north, to stay with my sister for the summer. It gets too hot here for the likes of us, doesn't it, Charlie?' She dips into her bag again and takes out a small electric fan. 'We're not even out of May yet and we're already struggling.'

She switches the fan on. It makes a soft whirring sound and blows her thin hair about. 'They say it's going to be hotter than ever this year, and last year nearly did for us, didn't it, Charlie? We don't want to go through that again, do we?'

Charlie looks up at Mrs Goldman with his big black button eyes. She tips some more water into his bowl and he's off again with the frantic lapping.

'You're in luck, we had a cancellation earlier. Saturday morning be OK?'

'Any chance you can squeeze me in tomorrow? We want to set off as soon as we can.'

I shake my head, say Friday's really busy, and she says not to worry, Saturday will be fine.

'We finish at one, so it'll be ready by then at the latest. We'll throw in a wax and polish too.'

Mrs Goldman scoops Charlie into her arms and kisses the top of its head. 'Isn't he a nice man, looking after us like that.'

All the while she fusses over Charlie, his eyes stay fixed on his bowl.

'Going north sounds like a good idea,' I say.

'My sister lives in Cumbria, near the coast, so we'll be able to cool off by the sea. You love the sea, don't you?' she says to Charlie. He flops down on the counter, splays his legs out and rests his head.

'It'll definitely be cooler but watch you don't get burnt. It's going to be an Amber Alert next week, even up north.'

She lifts Charlie up, takes hold of one of his paws and shakes it. 'What must we do? We must not get burnt. What must we do? We must not get burnt.'

'That's the way to do it.'

It comes out in my best Punch and Judy voice. Mrs Goldman stares at me with the same button eyes as Charlie. I feel the heat flare in my chest, feel it crawl up my neck into my face, feel it go all the way up to my hairline. I stand there blazing away like a mini sun and Mrs Goldman clutches Charlie to her chest. The door jangles as they leave. I pick up the dog bowl, tip what's left of the water over my head.

Only ten minutes to go until lunch time. I've brought my own today. Mum made me a sandwich. She wanted to use up the chicken. If anything's more than one day old it gets binned. No matter if it's been in the fridge. Mum doesn't trust the heat. I'm about to head off into the back room, get my sandwich from the fridge, when Malik appears with a black bin bag.

'That fruit of yours, I can stick it in with the rest of the rubbish if you want?'

I know it's a wind up. I know Malik knows better than to touch my things, but I still have to check. I still have to go see if the apples are still there. They are. All six of them. Still lined up on the sill. Still bathed in sunlight.

Malik chuckles to himself as he walks past. When he gets to the back door he stops.

'Weirdo,' he says, and steps out into the yard. He slams the door behind him and the window gives a sarcastic little rattle. I watch him cross to the workshop. He has to lower his head, use his hands for shade. There's no mercy this time of day. I look up at the bright blur of the sun.

'Another Ungrateful,' I say.

Celine's got dance mix bumping through the ceiling when I get home. I take the stairs two at a time. Barge straight in. Cross-legged on the bed, she hurls whatever she's holding at me. I duck, and something gets knocked off the shelf behind me. A small wooden elephant falls to the floor; it bounces on impact but the missile doesn't. I pick up the clay pipe, lay the broken halves on the duvet.

'You shouldn't smoke in the house.'

'Get lost.'

I move the pile of clothes off the chair next to the desk and sit down.

'What bit of "get lost" didn't you recognise?'

All her gear is arranged around her. Lighters, Rizlas, tobacco, hash, grass, spare pipe. She takes three Rizla papers and works them between her fingers. I sit and watch her roll a joint like a pro. She's good at it and she knows. When she's finished she sticks it in her mouth, takes a yellow lighter to the little bit of paper that's she twisted and flared. That's the bit I like to see.

I tell her it'll fuck her head up and she tells me she doesn't care.

'Everyone gets their head fucked by something or other. Least I'll enjoy it.'

Celine's room isn't what you'd call tidy and her desk is heaped with folders and files, gym kit, empty cans of drink, empty envelopes, bits of paper. I pick up a letter that's been opened. It's from school, addressed to Mum, about Celine's absences.

'Has Mum seen this?'

'Not yet,' she says, then carries on smoking.

'Are you smoking at school? You know she'll be the one who gets the penalty if you get caught.'

'I only smoke in the house, never outside. I'm not that stupid. Unless you plan on dobbing me in.'

She draws on her spliff, holds it for a second, then lets the smoke out in one long exhale. 'Mum wants the shed back. You need to ditch the dead zoo.'

She lifts the spliff to her mouth again, looks at me the way Malik does when he thinks he's being clever.

'When did she say that?'

'I heard her on the phone, talking.'

'What do you mean, talking? Talking about me?'

Celine shrugs.

I pick up a book from the desk, pretend to look through it. 'I'm doing important research, Mum knows that.'

'I'm just telling you what I heard.'

'Who was it? Who was she speaking to?'

Celine shrugs and I pick up the fallen elephant from the floor. I fire it and her hands fly up to shield her face and she knocks the spliff from her mouth. It drops onto the duvet and she jumps up, frantic. It's burnt a hole.

'It's a new fucking duvet, you arsehole!'

'How many times does she speak to him?' I ask. 'Anything. Anything you see, hear, you make sure you tell me. Do you hear me?'

'Fuck off and leave me alone!'

Celine flings her bedroom door open wide, waits for me to leave.

'You owe me a new duvet,' she says.

'I don't owe you anything. It's you who owes me, remember.'

She slams her door behind me and I go into my room. I lie down on the bed, open the drawer of the bedside table and take out the knife. You can't beat a Swiss Army knife for style and design. I let it rest in my palm. Love the colour. The shape. Love how it sits there. Heavy. Solid. Smooth. I tease each section open. Fan out the blades both sides to look like wings.

It's nearly half six and Mum will be finishing her shift soon. I ring her, tell her I'll pick her up from the tube at seven, save her legs. You've been standing all day, I say, and we can do a shop on the way back. She doesn't argue, sounds tired. I tell her I'll pick her up from Neasden.

She's waiting by the entrance when I arrive. I pull over. It's a no-stopping route and there's a white van behind, none too happy. Mum wastes time apologising to the van driver and as soon as she gets in I pull away. She witters about not having put her seat belt on. I give her a look and she doesn't moan anymore.

The North Circ's mad busy and I piss some drivers off by drifting too close. Mum makes annoying noises but knows better than to say anything. At Brent Cross we get stuck on the entry road, sit there for ages. I turn the radio up so Mum doesn't feel the need to fill the silence. I don't mind silence. It's smalltalk that gets me.

I manage to park up on the second level. When we step out of the car the heat hits us. That's the trouble with air con, it can exaggerate the heat, make you feel it's worse than it is, because your body needs time to adapt. Inside the shopping centre the air con is ultra-chilled. Too chilled sometimes. Seen people walking around in coats when it's mid-thirties outside.

When we get to the supermarket Mum gives me the list and her swipe card, and then sits at the small café opposite. I glance over as I head off with the trolley. She looks good in her uniform, navy and white suits her. She's still wearing her name badge though. It's not good, strangers knowing your name. I've told her but she doesn't listen. Forget how small she is, she looks like a doll sitting there, tips of her shoes don't even brush the floor.

Doll. That's what he used to call her. Cut her hair when she was asleep once, hacked one side of it clean off, like Celine did to Barbie.

The list isn't long and I'm done in half an hour. When I finish I push the half-full trolley towards the café. She's not there, the seat Mum was sitting in is empty. No sign of her in the other seats either. I spin the trolley round and nearly take out a buggy. The girl pushing it gives me a filthy look but the baby just grins.

I spot Mum at the far end of the mall, looking out the tinted plate glass. The sunlight streaming through the window is making her hair all golden and glittery. As I near she turns to face me and I see she's on her phone. She ends the call and grabs the trolley and heads off.

When we get to the car Mum stands, hands perched on the trolley like a bird. I point the keys, the lights flash and the doors release. We load in silence. When she's like this I don't know what to do, can't work out the clues. Don't know if she wants me to take the trolley back or what. Mum walks off with the trolley and smashes it into a stray. They waltz off into a bay meant for a car. I slam the boot shut and climb into the driver's seat.

'I'm driving.' She's like an air stewardess standing there in her work clothes, holding on to her shoulder bag, that tone in her voice. She holds her hand out for the keys.

'Thought you were tired,' I say.

'I'm not arguing about it.'

It's him. He can still screw things up, even though he's hundreds of fucking miles away. I get out and give Mum the keys. Soon as we've swapped seats Mum drives off. Want to put the radio on, listen to the weather forecast. Can't. Have to just sit here, be driven, but there's one thing I can do and that's think about tomorrow.

Mum tells me she's ordered blinds for my bedroom and I tell her I don't need any.

'You have to have something up at the windows, Luke.'

'I don't want anything at the windows, that's why I took the curtains down. It's my room. I'm the one sleeping in there.'

'If you draw the blinds in the day it'll stop the room heating up. Your room is like an oven, Luke, and you keep the air con on all night. I can't afford that expense. It's not good for you anyway.'

He's sucked it all up, like he always does. He's a black hole, that's what he is. A big fucking black hole. I lie back in my seat and watch the sun go into meltdown behind the buildings. Sweet, this time of day. Everything looks like it's been dipped into honey. Our road faces west and as Mum turns into it, the rays bounce off the bonnet straight in through the windscreen. It's blinding, like a flashlight. Mum loses control. I hear the tyres scrape the kerb as we thud to a halt.

'Bloody sun.' Mum's hands are rigid on the steering wheel. She looks at me, asks what's so funny.

'Why are you smiling?' she says.

'Don't blame the sun. *He's* the one got you all twitchy and nervy.

Was it him told you to get the blinds? Was it him told you not to let me drive home? I know you've been talking to him, don't try and deny it, Mum.'

'OK. I spoke to him but all we talked about was Celine's birthday, nothing else. He didn't talk about blinds and he didn't talk about you.'

'If we're stopping you need to stick your hazards on,' I say.

'Don't tell me what to do.'

'I'm surprised he remembered her birthday. How long's it been? Only eight years. Did you tell him she's all grown up now and a cuddly toy won't do it anymore?'

Mum starts the car, checks the mirror.

'That's why he rang, he wanted to know what to get her. I told him to put some money in a card.'

'He's sending her a card, you gave him our address? Please tell me you didn't do that. No way. No fucking way.'

Mum shakes her head and I thump the dashboard.

'He's her father, he's yours too. I can't ignore that fact and I can't ignore him forever.'

'Yes, you can. You have a choice.'

Mum checks her mirror again and indicates.

'He might come down for it. He might come down for Celine's birthday.'

I open the car door.

'You're so going to regret this,' I say and get out.

I walk the rest of the way. Mum passes me. I watch the car drive away and in the distance the waves of heat rising up from the road make it look like it's melting. They make it everything look like it's melting. What if that actually happened? What if it got so hot everything just melted, us included. Bet he wouldn't. Bet Dad wouldn't fucking melt.

Friday, 27th May 2022

I'm in the back room sitting at the coffee table, taking my morning break, when Malik comes in.

'I can help set you up with a girl.'

So fucking predictable.

'Good-looking guy like you, you should get yourself out, strut your stuff.'

He sits the wrong way round on his chair. Thinks it makes him look cool the way he straddles it, thinks because I don't talk about girls, because I don't talk about what I do, where I go, that he knows me.

'Man, you should get down to that new club in Neasden, plenty of flesh on show there.' He cracks on like I need tips, like I'm interested in what he's got to say. 'There was this piece the other week, Scarlet. Her name isn't the only thing hot about her, know what I'm saying.'

He lets out a whistle and holds on to the back of his chair. Bounces up and down as if he's riding it, then lets one hand whip free cowboy style. He stops and tells me how she was gagging for it, how she dragged him into the toilets and how a bouncer was banging on the door as they were banging away. When he's talking shit I run a loop in my head. DICK-KNOB-ARSE. DICK-KNOB-ARSE. DICK-KNOB-ARSE. Keep it going long as I can.

'Get yourself down there Saturday, tell her Malik sent you.'

He winks at me like I'm his mate, takes out a rag he keeps in the pocket of his overalls and wipes his face, smears oil all over it.

I tell him I've already got plans.

'Course you have, Lukey Boy. Lining up for you, aren't they?'

He stands up and walks over to the mirror above the sink, checks himself out.

'What have you got planned?' I ask.

'Wouldn't you like to know, Lukey Boy, wouldn't you like to know?'

I wouldn't. Not one bit interested, but I act like I am to keep the subject on him.

'Seeing Scarlet?'

He smirks. 'You should come out with me and the boys one night. Seriously, you'd have a good time.'

He flashes a cocky grin then struts off. Thinks he's a Bollywood star, even in his fucking overalls. Wouldn't occur to him I wasn't interested in his plans. Wouldn't occur to him that mine might be a lot more interesting.

I open the back door to the yard. It's a hint that break time is over but he hasn't finished preening himself.

'Man, you're letting the cool air out and the hot air in,' he says.

I step into the yard and close the door behind me. Topped forty degrees the other day. Lethal to leave doors and windows open now. They're saying it's the hottest May on record. Doesn't feel the same country, feels like we've been dragged kicking and screaming towards the equator. It's the stillness that does it. You don't see litter scuttling down the street anymore or coke cans rolling around in the gutter. Nothing dare move. Everything's too shit-scared the sun might decide to nuke them.

I look up at the sun, feel the heat on my face. This time of the morning it's bearable but you know it won't last long. Won't be able to stand here like this after midday. If the sun doesn't get you, the solar patrols will.

I walk over to the workshop. Mo's got his head stuck inside the guts of a BMW. He's a good worker. Never takes long breaks. Hardly takes any. Hard to believe they're brothers.

I hear the scuff of Malik's trainers behind me.

'You should be more careful,' he says. 'That pretty face of yours, it'll end up looking as rank as those apples. Why do you leave them to rot like that? You're fucking weird.'

I tell him to get back to work and leans against the car Mo's working on.

'Break's not over yet, five more minutes.'

I can't be bothered to argue with him. Meant to replace them with fresh this morning but I forgot. I wrap up the apples with some hand towels and put them in the bin. There's a constant stink comes out the bin. Malik says Kojak should supply us with a pedal bin but he won't, same as he won't supply us with decent air con or a water fountain. I can take that. Anything that gets under Malik's skin is alright by me.

I stand at the window and thank the sun for its mercy. I'm off tomorrow, I say, but I'll bring in new ones after the weekend.

Saturday, 28th May 2022

Love having a full weekend. Malik hates the fact I get one in four Saturday mornings off. Think he has more right to time off because he's got a life. I've got a life too but I don't need to shout about it. Don't want to shout about it, because then people would know, interfere, and that can't happen.

The sun wakes me about half five. It's the most natural way to wake up. The body was meant to be in sync with the seasons and the light. I'm so not putting any fucking blinds up because I know what will happen. Mum will want me to draw them. She'll nag me until I lose it with her. *What grown man sleeps with a light on and the curtains open?* I know she thinks I should have grown out of it by now. It's OK for a kid to be afraid of the dark but not an adult. It's not that simple though, and she knows it.

I hear Mum get up and take a shower. She must be on earlies. I lie there thinking about what I need to do today. Got enough roadkill, the shed's busting with it, but I could go hunting for scrap. Have a poke around, see what's new. Mum leaves and I get up. Celine won't stir for hours. I make myself a decent breakfast and check on the weather status.

The scrapyard's up past the Esso garage on the way to Neasden tube. A Sun Patrol passes me at the junction by the petrol station. It's an Amber Alert today so the mobile units are out and about in their bright red vans with their bright red suns. They used to be yellow but it made the sun look too friendly, now it looks like the devil spawn of a tomato and a starfish. I give the driver a wave as he checks me out. I'm in the recommended dress code – long sleeve t-shirt, loose fitting trousers, hat, sunshades – no reason for him to pull me over.

As I near the yard, a lorry-load of scrap thunders past and a cloud of dust follows. When it clears I see a four-wheel drive has come to a halt on the opposite side of the road. A woman is at the wheel, two screaming kids beside her. She gets out, walks to the front of the car and stares at the ground. She's wearing shorts and a short-sleeved top and I want to tell her how lucky she is to have just missed the mobile preachers. A queue of traffic builds up behind and someone in the tailback toots. The woman climbs back into her car, but before she gets a chance to move off a girl pushes past me, runs straight into the road.

'Stop. Stop. It's alive. It's still alive!' the girl shouts.

The woman grinds the car into gear and tries to wave the girl away but she's not having any, smacks her hands down on the bonnet. The kids go hysterical and the girl crouches down in front of the offside tyre. Her long blonde hair falls forward and she has to tuck it behind her ear.

'It's moving. It is. Look, it's moving!'

She looks over and fixes me with her eyes, pleads with me to do something. I should keep on walking, keep on going, carry on until I get to the scrapyard, but her eyes won't let me. I walk over, squat down beside her. There's a squirrel splayed out by the offside wheel. Its back legs are fucked and it's trying to drag itself along by its front paws. It would be better to let the car finish the job, put the animal out of its misery.

I slide my hand underneath the fur, feel the heart bounce in my palm. I lift it up and the squirrel blinks a black bead of an eye. Can feel soft neat ears against my skin. Can see miniature leather hands for paws. Slimmest, nimblest fingers ever. You'd expect the tail to be thick, bushy, but it's not, it's almost see-through it's that light.

We step onto the pavement and the woman accelerates away. The girl wants to take it to a vet, asks me if I know if there's one nearby. I tell her I don't. The squirrel's breathing too fast. I suggest moving into the shade and the girl shoves her phone in my face.

'Found one. It's only half a mile away, we could take it there now.

We could be there in a few minutes.'

She's looking at me all hopeful, showing me the Google map and the location of the vet and she's right, it isn't far, it's just over the road but it doesn't matter how near or far it is.

Frozen mid-breath, mid-twitch, it doesn't look real, looks fake, like a toy.

'Is it dead?'

I nod and even though she looks scared, even though her face is all tight with worry, she's stunning. Want to put my arms around her, tell her not to worry, tell her it'll be OK, tell her these things happen.

'What can we do? We can't just leave it here?'

'I'll take it home,' I say. 'Bury it in the garden.'

A smile flits across her face and it feels like the sun's come out from behind a cloud and changed everything. I'm standing there holding a dead squirrel, next to a girl I've never met before, and it feels fine. Feels more than fine. Feels fucking great.

'I should go,' she says, 'I'm already late.'

She picks her bag up and stands there backlit with sunlight. She's got this halo. She looks like an angel. Want to tell her that. Want to tell her I've never seen anyone like her before. Want to tell her she's beautiful.

She doesn't move, stands in front of me swinging her big hippy bag. There's a sentence at the back of my throat, it's a line I hear all the time on TV when some guy likes the look of a girl. All I have to do is roll it off my tongue but I swallow it instead.

She stops swinging her bag and walks away, easy as that. It feels like I've been winded. As if someone's taken me out. Suddenly the scrapyard isn't that appealing anymore. I pick up a discarded burger box from the forecourt of the garage. I tuck Fluffy inside, slip the made-to-measure coffin into my rucksack and follow her.

She takes the Northern line to Belsize Park. I make sure to keep a good distance, don't cross the main road until she turns off by the town hall. She carries on down Belsize Avenue, turns right and cuts through a maze of smaller streets. The roads here are all the same, big-fronted, bay-windowed terraces. All brass knockers and letterboxes and shiny numbers.

I'm thirsty as fuck. I dig around in my rucksack for some water and lose sight of her. Think I've missed her going into a house but then I spot her standing on a doorstep, the only house with its number painted in white on the brickwork. She rummages in her bag for her keys and has to tuck her hair behind her ears to stop it getting in the way. She finds the key, unlocks the door and goes inside. I get a last glimpse of her in the hallway before the door slams shut.

I kneel down behind a 4x4 and think of my next move. Thought I'd be able to walk straight up, knock on the door, say that sentence. Now it doesn't seem that easy. She might think I'm weird, following her all the way from Neasden like that, might not even remember me. Malik would know what to do. He's a dickhead but he wouldn't let someone like her get away.

I tear a page out of my notebook, scribble my name and number on it, fold it over and address it to 'Squirrel Girl'. As I push it through the letterbox I try not to let it snap back but I'm not quick enough. On the tube home I suck at my knuckle, think about her. I think about her all day. I'm still thinking about her when I go to bed. I think how mad it all was. The car, the squirrel, me following her home, me putting the note through her door. I'm wondering if she'll read it, whether I'll ever see her again, when my phone rings.

'Hi.'

I can't breathe, let alone speak.

'Luke?'

I manage to say hi back. There's music and people talking in the background and her reply gets drowned out by a blast of heavy metal. She says it again.

'It's me, Squirrel Girl!' She shouts it loud and a hundred thousand balloons burst inside my head. The music gets turned down and this time I hear her, feels like she's right here, right next to me.

'What you up to?'

I take my hand out of my boxers and sit up. 'Nothing.'

'I'm at a party. Wanna come over?' she asks.

The sound of her voice is such a turn on. My whole body feels like it's been stuffed into a power socket. It's Saturday, it's ten past ten. She's at a party and I'm in bed, at ten past fucking ten on a Saturday.

'I… I'm… well… I'm.'

I try and think of something to say.

'Sorry, bit out of it,' she slurs. 'Just wanted to ring to say thanks, you know, for the note and for your help with everything. And that I really… well I was really surprised, but pleased, about the note and l think. Well, I think you're—'

She stops and all I can hear is giggling and shrieking. Then another voice, male, shouts down the phone.

'Fee thinks you're fit, really fit, as in exceptionally fit.'

There's more shrieking and then Fee steals my line.

'Do you want to meet up, go for a coffee or something?'

I say sure but she doesn't hear me, so I shout it as loud as I can.

'Great, ring me in the morning and we'll sort something.'

I say cool and then the phone goes dead. She doesn't just think I'm fit, she thinks I'm *really* fit. That's what he said. He said Fee thinks you're really fit.

Fee.

I say her name out loud. Sounds like a whisper, a secret.

Sunday, 29th May 2022

The alarm wakes me. I try and smack the snooze button but I'm twisted up in the sheets like a toffee. I wriggle around, tear them away and scramble to my feet. I stand on the bed, legs shaking, heart banging.

I'm standing naked in front of the window, but I don't care because it's still there. Still screwed into the top right-hand corner, still blazing away like a 1000w bulb. Someone across the way opens their window, it catches the light, sends a laser beam right at me. I fall backwards onto the bed, laughing like a psycho who's just been taken off death row.

I lift my head up and see the burger box on the floor by my rucksack. The squirrel, the girl, it happened. Everything fucking happened. The sun isn't dead, it didn't go out. And I met a girl. A girl called Fee.

I get dressed, take Fluffy downstairs with me. Hear the buzzing soon as I open the door. I try and bat them out of the way. One gets in my mouth. Soggy flies for breakfast wasn't on the menu. I spit it out and push the shed door open wide as it'll go. I've told Mum and Celine to keep out, told them to keep away, but someone's not been listening to me. Someone's been in and shut the shed window. It needs to be left open to let any flies escape. Roadkill isn't clean, there's always eggs waiting to hatch, and in this heat they hatch quick.

I swat the last one out, close the shed door. There's only the two recent carcasses on the table, a fox cub and a pigeon. The mice and the rat have gone. Mum's got rid of them. She shouldn't look through the window. I keep telling her not to. At least there's plenty of room for Fluffy. I lie the squirrel down. Rigor mortis has set in and the tail's the only fluffy thing about it.

I suggested Marine Ices in Chalk Farm. It's not that far from where Fee lives. As soon as I said it I thought it sounded naff, like we were a couple of kids or something, but she loved the idea. We're not meeting till one so I've got all morning to check on the stats. The true stats, not the fake stats. Not the stats they trot out to keep up the pretence.

I eat my breakfast at my PC. Chew on burnt toast as I scroll through all the data. I need to transfer the latest results from my notebook to the spreadsheet but I get diverted before I can. A popup catches my eye. It's from an Unbeliever site called *Climate Change What Climate Change*. They changed their name a year ago and at the time I sent them a message saying I preferred the original one but it bounced back with a this-site-has-blocked-you autoreply. I used another login and said it wasn't good to block people who had different views.

They blocked that too, so I made up another. I click on the popup.

Professor Hannah Jefferson can reveal that the latest government data regarding the global warming crisis has been deliberately tampered with to hide several inconsistencies. The data is therefore skewed and should be regarded as invalid. The suggestion that global warming is accelerating towards a Dante's Inferno model is therefore unfounded and should be treated with the utmost scepticism.

I skip most of the article, it's full of the usual – *natural phenomena, temperatures will always peak then cool, global warming just a tactic to divert attention pressing from more problems.* What, like maybe watering the desert that is California, stopping Australia becoming one big fucking bushfire?

I click on a Believer site. Good to check in on those clowns too. The topic today is individual responsibility. *Global warming is as much a micro problem as a macro problem. Everyone needs to be mindful. Fossil fuels, carbon emissions, ozone thinning...*

I click on a forum and scroll down to see a post I actually agree with. Last_snowcrystal says while they fully support the government line, and agree global warming is happening, they disagree with the rationale behind the conclusion. Sometimes taking a historic view of events is useful to throw light on a future problem.

I clap my hands together. Someone's thinking along the same lines as me. I post a reply. Say I'm of the same opinion and that I've got a theory of my own and I'd like to know more about what they have to say.

As I scroll further, Last_snow_crystal replies to my post.

Message to Saviour: No one here supports your theories. Least of all me. I left that comment as bait and you bit. Shows what you really are. A sap. Keep your mad thoughts to yourself, you're not welcome on this forum or any forum.

Know who it is straight away. The shithead troll that took a disliking to me because I threatened his standing. Threatened his authority. Believer22356 aka Last_snowcrystal aka Shitforbrains.

I get to Chalk Farm with fifteen minutes to spare. I wait inside the entrance, near the big industrial fan. London's answer to the heat crisis is to stick mega sized fans everywhere but only Zone 1 and 2 tube stops have them. They're not much good at cooling anything, all they do is blow hot air at you. The walls of the station are covered in shiny brown tiles that look like huge slabs of toffee. Dad's local had the same tiles. I'd press my face against them and count to twenty before I went in, before I told him he had to come home. He always made me wait, and then he'd kick me all the way home because his dinner, our dinner, everyone's dinner would be ruined.

I check the time. Maybe she said half one, maybe the party was an all-nighter, maybe she slept in or maybe she met someone else. I'm in shirt and shorts and I've got a stupid baseball cap stuck on my head. I should have worn something else, something more hip. All the anti-UV gear is in now — baggy trousers, loose shirts, lightweight hoodies, even kaftans. Not sure I'd carry off a kaftan but Malik would. He'd be standing here looking like a fucking supermodel.

I take my cap off and try to funk up my hair but it's way too short. Hate it when it's just been cut. At least my shades are new. I tell myself she thinks I'm fit anyway. She didn't actually say it though, it was her mate. Maybe he was joking, maybe that's what they were laughing at. Maybe that's where she is now, with him. Maybe this is all a wind up. She's twenty-eight minutes late now. If she doesn't show in ten, I'll go. Maybe that's how it is. The world's divided up between those that get and those that don't.

Fee turns up thirty seconds later. She's got that bleary-eyed, bedhead thing going on and I don't care how late she is, she could be two hours, two days, two fucking weeks, I don't care because she's here, looking even more beautiful than I remembered. I get a kiss on the cheek. She smells of shampoo but there's a hint of tobacco as her lips brush my face. What's weird is that I hate cigarettes, hate smokers, but the stale scent coming from her mouth makes me want to cover it with mine.

She pushes her shades up and I lift mine too and we stand there checking each other out. She's got on a thin floaty top covered in beads and sparkly things and bracelets, lots of bracelets. The hippy chick look suits her.

'Sorry I'm late,' she says.

I say it's OK and start to walk on.

'Wait up, I need to fix this hair.'

She gives me her glasses to hold and throws her head forward, shakes her hair to the floor. There's a row of kiss curls at the nape of her neck and I get this urge to touch them but she flicks her head back up. Her hair's become a wild thick mane. She looks like a lion and I feel like her prey. She smiles at me, slips her arm through mine and we walk off down the road like boyfriend and girlfriend, like we're a proper couple.

It's packed. Fee tells me it always is.

'Camden celebs hang out here. I've seen tons.' She says some names but I've no idea who she's talking about.

We have to wait to be seated and I don't know what to say but Fee's busy checking out who's in and who's not. Finally, we get shown to our seats by the window. We sit down opposite each other and she smiles at me again and this time I notice she's got a small gap between her front teeth. It suits her. Just like the kiss curls do.

There's no menu so I reach over and grab one from the next table.

'Did you bury the squirrel?' Fee asks.

I nod and look at the menu.

'She was speeding, you know. It makes me sick how people think they can do that. Run over an innocent animal who was just going about its business.'

She sounds cross, the kind of cross a kid gets when they can't have any sweets.

'To be fair, there wouldn't have been much time to brake,' I say.

Cross face turns to angry face and I can't believe I've fucked up already.

'But you're right, she should have been going slower,' I add.

She grabs the menu off me, tells me she's got a hangover and sulks behind it. Yesterday I thought she looked round about my age but today she seems nearer Celine's. I wonder if I should ask how old she is. If that's a conversation starter or a conversation ender.

'Ice cream's a good cure for a hangover,' I say.

She calls me a liar and then she does this thing with her left eyebrow. Arches it, real slow, real sexy. The waiter arrives to take our order and Fee orders an orange and lemon sorbet and I have a Knickerbocker Glory. As soon as I say it I wish I hadn't. She's the one ordering a grown-up dessert and I've gone for the kids' choice.

She finishes before me. We haven't said a word since we started eating and I know she's waiting for me to say something, and I know I should. I wonder whether I should go with my question about how old she is, just to get the conversation started but before I get a chance she dumps a bucketload my way. She wants to know my favourite band, favourite food, favourite colour, favourite place to hang out. When I tell her I don't do bands she pulls a shocked face.

'Do you do girlfriends?'

I drop my gaze, stare at the table.

'How many have you had?'

I feel my neck burning and I wish I hadn't come. I look at how far away the door is and think about saying I need to go to the loo and just leaving.

'OK, I'll go first, get it over with.' She counts on her fingers. 'Josh, Ali, Tom-Tom, Egg Man, Jake.'

She makes a high five and I try and pick a number. Two. I decide two sounds reasonable but the way she looks at me when I say it, makes me wish I'd said more.

'What you doing next week?'

'Working.'

'Where?'

'In a garage.'

'Can you take time off?'

'Why?'

'I thought maybe…' She scrapes the dregs that have sunk to the bottom of her glass, with her spoon. 'Maybe, we could spend some time together.' She licks the spoon and adds, 'At yours.'

Thought about her non-stop. Thought about how she might look with her kit off. Imagined kissing her. Doing it with her. And now she's offering and all I can think about is me lying beside her. Her, five lovers. Me, a virgin. The word fills my mouth, makes me cough.

'Well.'

I cough again and tell her it's not a good time, that the garage is mega busy and my boss wouldn't let me have time off.

'Shame.'

That's all she says but my balls physically shrink.

'Actually, I didn't do it with all of them, so really, it's only Tom-Tom and Jake that count. If there's no sex you can't really say you're boyfriend and girlfriend, can you?'

She hums to herself and looks around. What is she saying? Is she telling me if we don't do it soon, then she's not interested in me?

'Let me see what I can do. I might be able to take the Wednesday off,' I say.

Kojak won't like it but Celine will be at school and Mum's on ten till six that day, so the house will be ours.

'Cool.' Her eyebrow seals the deal and I wonder if I could ring Kojak now and ask for the time off. I finish the rest of my ice cream.

'I can't believe you followed me all the way home and I didn't even see you,' Fee says. 'You're not a cop, are you?'

When she asks that I snort ice cream down my nose and she yells out I've got pink snot running down my face. It sends her hysterical and it feels good to make her laugh. She passes me a serviette and I wipe the ice cream away and then I put on a serious face and a serious voice.

'Actually, I am, and I need to talk about a crime you witnessed. It involved a small furry animal.'

She laughs louder this time and I frown and wag my finger.

'That's really not very nice, Miss, we talkin' homicide after all. We talkin' first degree murder.'

I say moider for murder and Fee jumps in, bats a line right back in a much better accent.

'Will you need to take me in for questioning, officer?'

'That's very likely, Miss.'

'Will you need to search me, officer?'

She waits for the return but I haven't got one. I go back to eating my ice cream and there's a lull that threatens to turn into one of those silent bombs. It's a shame because I was doing so well, so much better than I thought I'd do.

'And your favourite book is?'

I'm glad she's talking but I wished she'd asked me something else.

'There's so many, isn't there,' she carries on. 'Think my all-time favourite is, and I know it's corny and boring, but it just has to be *To Kill a Mockingbird*. I'm guessing you're a fan of sci-fi or fantasy. Am I right?'

'I don't read,' I say, and her jaw drops open in mock horror.

'I mean I do read, I can read, I just don't read novels, fiction. I'm not that kind of reader. I only read stuff that interests me.'

She shrugs herself forward. 'And what interests Luke?'

I think about telling her. Giving her the facts. The true facts, not the false facts, not the lies everybody buys into.

'You,' I say.

She smiles and then she talks about herself. She tells me she's an only child, lives with her Mum, her Dad lives abroad, she doesn't see much of him but he keeps in touch.

'I don't see my Dad at all,' I say but she's not listening.

She tells me she lives in Belsize Park and that her Mum is away a fair bit, so she spends a lot of time on her own. I ask how old she is.

'Sixteen. I don't mind living at home alone, I can take of myself.'

She sits up, brushes her hair back from her face and I can tell this is not a windup. She's got that confidence, that self-belief, it shines right out of her.

'I'm a year ahead so I can take my A levels next year and then I'm going to apply to Oxbridge. I'll need to work really hard next year, so this year I'm making sure I get in as much fun as possible.'

She looks at me like no girl has ever looked at me before and all I can think about is that she's off to uni and all I got was one GCSE.

'You're going to uni at seventeen?' I ask.

'Sure am. What were you doing at seventeen? And how old are you, by the way?'

I say I'm nineteen and I don't bother answering the other question.

Fee leans back in her chair and folds her arms. I know this is my cue to say something but I'm not sure what. I ask if she's got any brothers and sisters and she reminds me she's an only child. I tell her I've got one sister and Fee picks up her mobile phone from the table and sits there checking it. A heaviness sinks through me, pins me to the seat.

In the end we both speak at once. She asks what my sister's called, at the same time as I tell her, it's like we've read each other's minds and the heaviness disappears.

'Younger or older?' Fee asks.

'She's fourteen, be fifteen soon.'

'Is she having a party?'

'No idea.'

'Find out, maybe we could go.'

She's smiling at me like she means it and I smile back at her, can't stop. My mouth feels like it never wants to do anything else.

'To be honest I don't really have much to do with her. She does her thing and I do mine.'

'What about your Mum?'

'Same, really.'

'Your Dad?'

'Haven't seen him since I was eleven.'

'You not close to any of them?'

'Nope.'

'Nothing wrong with that. What about friends? You a bit of a loner? It's OK, I like oddballs, outsiders and I know the perfect book you should read, *The White Colt*.'

She gets all excited, tells me it's about a boy who doesn't fit in, about how lonely that makes him feel but then he meets a man who has a horse that needs looking after.

'They have this connection. It's life-changing, the horse gives him something to live for. Found it in a charity shop, remind me to lend it to you.'

Fee needs to get back, her hangover's caught up with her. I pay at the till and we walk back to the tube. This time when we hold hands I don't feel it's pretend. She stands in front of the toffee tiles, swinging her bag like she does and we both lean forward at the same time and bang noses. We manage a few quick pecks on the lips and she makes a 'text me' gesture as she heads down the stairs to the platform. I shout OK a bit too loud.

On the bus home she beats me to it.

– *Had a great time XXX*

I text back.

– *Snap*

– *Can't wait to meet again XXX*

Before I can tap out my reply she sends me another.

- *Wed?*
- *Will try*
- *Really like you XXX*
- *Like you too X*
- *XXXXXXXXXXXXXXXXXX*

I count the number of kisses. Nineteen. One for each year.

Wednesday, 1st June 2022

Kept wishing I could fast forward, skip right past Monday and Tuesday, but now it's here, now I'm standing in the kitchen making my last breakfast as a virgin, I keep switching from feeling so happy I could combust, to feeling so fucking scared I want to vomit. An oldie comes on the radio, 'All You Need is Love', and I catch myself whistling as I spread butter on my toast.

'Someone's in a good mood.'

Mum's beside me in the kitchen.

'Got the day off,' I say.

'You never said.'

'Sorry, I didn't know I was supposed to check it with you first.'

'You got an interview for another job?'

'Nope, just fancied a day off, that's all.'

Mum moves away, walks over to the fridge and takes out her packed lunch that she prepared last night.

'I'm on a double shift today so you'll need to do tea and make sure Celine eats something,' she says as she walks into the lounge.

I leave at my usual time, wear my usual clothes. I tell Mum to have a good day and walk off down the road. I only said it to wind her up. She hates that phrase. Says there's no such thing as a good day when you're working it. I'm with her on that. A good day for me is coming back with a rucksack full of roadkill. A great day when I spend time doing tests and an excellent day is one where I get results, confirmation. True facts don't lie, they got no reason, got nothing to gain or lose. Unlike people. People lie all the time. Powerful people, they're the worst, they lie the most because they've got the most to lose.

We're not meeting until ten so I go and sit in the café opposite the tube. I buy an iced tea and sit near the window so I can keep a look out. Can't keep still, keep getting up to go to the loo. The third time I do the guy behind the counter throws me a look so I leave. A mobile unit has parked up on the pavement outside the tube station and a medic in a white coat jumps me.

'How are you today? Do you mind if I ask you a few questions? Have you had one of our leaflets?'

I try and walk on but she blocks me.

'Could you tell me when you last had your skin checked?'

'Last week,' I say.

She hands me a leaflet. 'We're offering walk-in screening today if you've time for another one.'

I fold the leaflet in half, stick it in my back pocket.

'We have dermatologists on site, free sun cream, won't take long.'

I say no thanks and head off.

'Remember. Slap it on. Cover up. Stay safe,' she shouts.

'From what?' I shout back.

'Skin cancer has risen by three hundred percent. Global warming has made the sun's effects much more harmful. The sun can be extremely dangerous, you should never underestimate it.'

'The sun or global warming, which is it?'

She looks confused. 'Sir, you can't argue with the facts, the increased statistics have coincided with the increase in global warming.'

'You can argue, and people are,' I say.

'I really think you should step inside and have a full body check. I can already see you've got signs of sun damage. You should be following the recommended advice. There's information in our leaflets and on our website, but I would urge you to step inside and take up the offer.'

I take the leaflet out of my back pocket and tear it up. 'Think I'll pass.'

'We're here all day,' the medic says. 'If you change your mind.'

She thinks I'm an Unbeliever. Thinks I don't believe in global warming. I'm not. They're following the wrong scent, just as much as the Believers are. And while they're both too busy mistrusting each other, they can't see what's going on right in front of them.

I pace up and down at the entrance. A ticket inspector clocks me so I go wait by the turnstile. He keeps on watching me until Fee strolls through, then all he can do is look at her.

Want to go to her, but my legs that wouldn't stay put a few minutes ago won't move at all now. Fee walks up to me and kisses me, full on the mouth. Does it right in front of the guard, everyone. Then she takes my hand and skips into the street.

'Do you mind if we grab a coffee? Only I didn't have time this morning,' she says.

'No. I mean, no, I don't mind. Not no, I don't want to. I do. I do want to go for a coffee.' Right now I'd do anything she wanted. I'd walk right up to the ticket inspector and the medic and punch them both if she asked me.

We go back into the café I've just left. The guy behind the counter gives me a different look now. Fee orders two cappuccinos, one with extra topping for her. She eats up all the chocolatey bits with a teaspoon, holds the last spoonful out for me. I shake my head, but then she does that trick with her eyebrow. I tried to do it in the bathroom this morning but couldn't. I open my mouth and take the spoonful of froth and chocolate. When she pulls the spoon back out she does it real slow and that fear, the one that was there earlier, the one that had me pacing up and down while I was waiting for, it wakes up again.

'Are you a virgin?'

Never met anyone as straight-talking as her. Never met anyone that says exactly what they think like she does.

'It doesn't matter, we can go back to yours and chill, sit and listen to music if you want. We don't have to do anything, we can just be together. You and me.'

I like how she says you and me. Like how she makes three words sound so fucking special.

She wraps her arm around my waist when we leave the café and leans into me. It feels like I've found a piece of a jigsaw that I didn't know was missing and it's slotted into place, and suddenly there it is, the whole picture.

We make out all the way back to my house.

On the bus. Off the bus.

In the street. In the house.

Up the stairs. On the bed.

33

It's good on the bed. We kiss until our mouths get dry then Fee whispers we should take our clothes off. We tear at our clothes like they're on fire, fling them everywhere and then we both dive under the duvet and I catch a flash of breasts and legs. It's such a rush when we touch. Such a rush to feel her skin. She runs her hands up and down my back, and we kiss some more. I put my hands on her breasts and she bites my neck. I'm ready and she knows. She whispers she wants me but soon as I start thinking about my next move the fear wakes up again, and all I can see is my pale scrawny body next to her perfect one and everything stops.

Want her to go. Want her to get dressed, get out and never speak to me again. Want to forget her. Want to forget this. Want to pretend it never happened. I'm nineteen and I'm still a virgin. And that's how it's going to stay.

Fee snuggles up to me, kisses my shoulder and tells me it's OK. It's anything but OK. I'm nineteen and I'm a virgin and that's how it's going to stay.

'I like tattoos,' she says. 'I think they're sexy.'

She's saying it to make me feel better but all it does is annoy me. My tattoo isn't there to be sexy. Now I've got fear and anger sitting inside of me and that's not a good mix. Fee runs her tongue over my shoulder blades, traces the image out. She's doing it to get me hard again but it's not working. I tell her to stop and she gets up from the bed. I've got a fit, naked girl in my room. A naked girl who wants to have sex with me and I've given her the fucking brush-off.

'You know what I think? I think we should take a nice cool bath together,' she says.

I run a cold bath and Fee lowers herself into it, sticks her head straight under the water. Her hair fans out behind her. Looks darker when it's wet. She wouldn't suit being dark. I like the fact she's fair, like me. I step in and she pulls herself up to sitting. Water runs off her face, her shoulders, her breasts. Her nipples are amazing. Big brown circles with little pink teats.

She hunches her legs up as I sit myself down at the other end of the bath. She tells me to lie back and open my legs, then lays herself on top of me, so she's facing the ceiling. The water slaps against the side of the bath as we jiggle around to get comfy. I like the weight of her. I like how she folds my hands in front of her. We stay that way a while, then I kiss the top of her head. Her hair feels like silk against my lips. She tilts her head back and I see her tits. I move my hand over one, brush the nipple. That gives me a hard-on.

She giggles and her body shifts and rubs my dick against my leg. I jump and she twists around to look at me. Her eyes are two-tone. There's a ring of navy-blue around her pupil but the iris is as blue as the sky.

She turns her head away and plays with her hair, twists a wet strand round and round her finger. I push myself forward to sit up and she has to sit up as well. Strands of hair cling to her shoulders. I try and pick them up but they're stringy and slimy as seaweed. I tell her that, tell her her hair looks like seaweed and she pushes all her weight right back at me. I slam into the shampoos and conditioners lined up behind me. The bottles fall into the water and onto the floor. She laughs and I grab her, pull her round so she's facing me.

Her lips are marshmallow. I slide my tongue between her teeth and the tip finds hers. We flip positions. When she's beneath me, she brings her legs up around my hips. I trace my fingers all the way down her belly to her hairline. She pushes my hand further, arches her back and takes hold of my dick.

We both hear it at the same time. The key in the front door, the scrunch as it scrapes across the rug as it opens. I hear the footsteps on the stairs and clear the bath, make it to the door just before they come to a halt outside. I slip the lock, watch the handle twist up and down, up and down.

'Who's in there?'

It's Mum. My dick's in full salute and Fee has to bite her finger to keep quiet. Mum twists the handle again and I feel her weight against the door.

'Me, who do you think?' I shout. It comes out strained, like I'm having a shit.

I lean against the door and my dick points at Fee. I can tell she's impressed. She can't take her eyes of it.

'You going to be long?' Mum asks. 'I need a pee.'

I tell her I'm having a bath.

'I've just run it, sorry. Thought you were at work all day?'

'They put me on split shift. Sarah didn't come in.'

'Who's Sarah?' Fee mouths.

I shrug, thrust my hips at her and wiggle my dick about.

'Don't worry I'll go to Brent Cross, pick your blinds up, use the loos there. But you're helping me put them up tonight.'

I say OK and Mum's feet pit pat down the stairs. I hear the

scrunching sound of the front door and a few seconds later the stutter of the engine as it catches. As Mum drives away I hold a towel out for Fee. She stands up in the bath, wraps it around herself and holds out her hand.

'Don't go all shy on me now,' she says. She leads me out of the bathroom to the landing and Fee pushes the bedroom door open.

'Meant to ask, what's with all the graffiti and the imagery?'

She points at the far wall, at the numbers and diagrams that are scribbled all over it.

I sit next to her and my thigh touches her thigh. Her leg is half the size of mine and it's completely hairless.

'It's my workings out.'

'Ever thought about getting a white board?'

'It's easier to re-paint the wall.'

'You a mad professor? Oh my God, you are, you've let me go on about going to Cambridge, Oxford, and you're a fucking maths genius.'

'They're sums, that's all. Basic equations.'

'I see trigonometry and algebra.'

'I have to work out distances, timings and predictions.'

She looks around the room, at the posters and calendars on the other walls.

'It's all to do with the same thing,' I explain. 'I study the sun. It's my hobby.'

She looks at one of the posters with several different stages of the sun. She reads the box of text next to it and I tell her it's showing the sun's birth and death. She moves on to the next one.

'Is that your tattoo?' she asks.

'Mine's a Mayan sun god, that's an Aztec sun god. The Aztecs worshipped the sun too, believed it was our protector and that it was the place you went after death.'

'That's going to be one hot place to go. Speaking of heat, can you put the air con on, I'm literally burning up just looking at everything in here. You included.'

She puts her arms around me and tells me to kiss her.

Always thought my first time would be a bit of a fumble in the jungle. All this wildlife I'd never seen before, wouldn't know which bits to attack first and if your dick's not in the mood then what? It's not like you can strap a splint on it. Or worse, it decides to bottle it half way through. Or much much worse, it's over in seconds.

But it wasn't like that. Fee was as nervous as me at first. Could tell by the way she couldn't stop giggling. I was glad of that. Glad we could laugh about stuff. But I was glad she wasn't a virgin either. I'm ready for you, she went. I thought it'd be a struggle but she went on top, lowered herself down. Was weird how her body fit, like it was made for mine. It was slow at first but we soon got into a rhythm. Don't think I disappointed, not from the way she was digging her nails in.

All she had to do was touch me. Every nerve. Every muscle. Didn't need anything else. But the tattoo turned her on. She wants to get one done, similar to mine, said it would bond us. And she loved the posters, thought the sun icons were really cool and the Mayan calendars. She told me she loved Mexican culture. Aztecs, Nandos, she went. I like that about her. How she can do flippant but in a way that doesn't make me feel stupid, makes me feel she understands, makes me feel she gets me.

There's a fly crawling across the ceiling. It buzzes around the room and then goes back to crawling across the ceiling. Keeps doing it. Flies are underestimated. They can walk upside down *and* fly. Two superpowers in a thing that size.

Fee wakes and slides her arm across my chest. The sun falls in through the window, in a block of light, like it always does on a sunny day but this time it frames us both, pours its blessing on me, and Fee

Fee's found a chest hair. She tugs it and it stings. I slap her arse and we roll around and then I straddle her. Want to taste every bit of her. Eat every piece. I rub my palms over her breasts, her nipples harden and we do it again. I feel like I've got a superpower now. I feel like I could do anything. Be anything. Could fly to the sun and back. Could take Fee with me. Want to take her with me.

No one tells you about this. How it makes you feel.

How it really makes you feel.

Thursday, 2nd June 2022

Thought about her non-stop. Kept replaying everything. Her naked, us having sex, the way she looked at me when she said goodbye. We didn't want to let go of each other. I took a picture inside my head. Kept it there after she left There's this bond between us now. Me and her against the world. I know that wherever she is, whatever she's doing, I'm hers and she's mine. There was a girl at school that I liked but I didn't have the guts to do anything about it. She was pretty, but her eyes were too far apart. Only a bit, not much, but it made a difference. There's a formula. A computer somewhere has worked out what makes a perfect face. Fee's eyes fit it, everything about her fits.

Mum shouts up the stairs. 'Luke, I'm off, don't forget to double lock the door, Celine's not here, she's on a sleepover and don't forget, you're helping me put your blinds up tonight.'

Mum slams the door behind her and I kneel on the bed and look out the window at the sun. It's hidden behind a soft white cloud and it's turned the clouds a soft yellow, given it a golden edging.

'Mum wants to shut you out, but don't worry, that's never going to happen. No one's ever going to do that. Not even Fee. I hope you liked her. I think she understands and I think she's special.'

It feels like I've found a pot of fucking gold at the end of the fucking rainbow. I used to believe in that when I was a kid. Thought I'd come across my very own treasure once. Was out walking with the Cadets in the Peak District. Had to do ten miles with a heavy load. We'd stopped for a quick break and I had a carton of juice and a banana. After I'd eaten the banana I tried to bury the skin. Dug into the ground with my knife but that was the first of the long hot summers. There'd been weeks and weeks of dry weather. The ground was like fucking cement. Up near Mam Tor you get these huge boulders lying about, random style, like they've been dumped by a giant. There were two the size of car and a third one the size of a old-fashioned TV. I rolled the smaller one away so I could hide the banana skin and underneath there was this mad panic. Ants, beetles, worms, earwigs; all wriggling, writhing, charging into and over each other. That's when I saw it.

You could see what it was straight off, even though it was half buried. Thought it was old money at first; a shilling, sixpence, something like that. It was old all right. Horse and rider on one side, emperor on the other. Couldn't stop looking at it. Used to take it out and turn it over every five seconds. It was a Roman coin. And it was mine. Kept it a secret for nearly two weeks and then I let it slip to Celine. I was babysitting her, and she was kicking off so I showed it her to shut her up. Should have known she'd go telling tales. Told Dad soon as she saw him. Stupid bastard didn't have a clue. Sold it to a mate, got sweet FA for it. I'm not sharing Fee with anyone. No one's getting a chance to steal her away.

I text Fee on the way into work. Send her a heart emoji. When I get there I turn off my phone and make sure to keep out of Malik's way. He's too much of a sniffer dog, know straight away what I've been up to. I can actually smell it on me. Happiness stinks. It fucking stinks and I fucking love it.

The morning's slow, only two bookings. An air con malfunction and a dodgy handbrake. The only other distraction is Irish. He rings up on the hour, every hour. Kojak doesn't want to take his calls so I have to cover for him, which winds Irish up because he knows I'm lying. When he rings the fifth time I ask where he's from. I try and explain that sometimes he doesn't sound Irish.

'That's because I'm not. I'm Scottish. When I moved from Glasgow to London they couldn't tell the difference and the name stuck. Satisfied?'

'I didn't mean to pry,' I say.

'I don't go asking where you're from, but I know you're not a Londoner. While we're being straight there's no need for the bullshit, I know Kojak's there and I know why he's ignoring me, but you tell him from me, that's not how it works.'

Kojak pops his head out of his office, tells me to put the call through.

'You're in luck, he's just walked in, Irish, I'll put you through.'

I transfer the call, cut him off mid-swear, and then I nip across to Carlas. Carlas Sandwich Bar doesn't have an apostrophe and there was a bloke once who thought it was clever to ask how many Carlas there were. Kept going on about wanting to meet them all. He thought it was funny but Carla didn't. Carla doesn't find anything funny. She's got this stare when she gives you your food, it says now give me your money and do one. When the bloke offered to put in the apostrophe she spat in his salami and coleslaw sarnie, right in front of him, then threw it at him. I make sure I'm ready with my order, say it loud and clear because I don't want her spitting in my food.

I join Mo in the back room. We always eat our lunch together, sitting around the coffee table. Carla always puts my lunch inside a paper bag and gives me a paper plate. This is what we do every day. I eat my sandwich off a paper plate and Mo eats out of a plastic tub. It's the same thing every day. Naan bread and curry. Once he had a bhaji and spinach as extra and he was so fucking excited.

We don't ever say much and I'm too scared to say anything today in case I let it slip about Fee but I feel I should say something because I don't know that much about Mo. I know he's Malik's brother, and he likes eating curry, and that he's a good honest worker, but that's about it.

I ask him if he likes working here and it sounds like I'm giving him a job appraisal, but Mo doesn't seem to find it a strange thing to ask over lunch.

'It's good to work, everyone needs to work. I am happy when I work, really I am.'

I believe him, even though I know he's saying it in the hope it gets back to Kojak. Everything he does is to impress Kojak.

Mo shoves two fingers in the air. 'Two,' he goes. 'Been here two years.'

'Snap,' I say.

'We are twins, twins of garage, and me... I am oldest.'

For some reason, he finds this really funny. Gurns his lips back and laughs out loud. He's got a proper gummy smile and really pink gums. Pink as shrimp sweets. I tell him that. Tell him his sugar pink gums remind me of sweets.

'Teeth-rotting sweets,' I add.

'My teeth are good because I don't eat sweets and I don't drink Coke.'

He's making a sly dig at Malik and I like that. I ask if he's ever been out with Malik and he shakes his head.

'You're not like him, are you?' I ask. 'It's OK, you don't have to be like him.'

'I only came here four years ago. I was brought up in India. Malik was brought up here. We don't share a common childhood.'

I feel an idiot for not knowing that.

'Do you miss India?'

'I used to, but now the weather here reminds me of home. Feels like I'm back in India, the heat, the rain. Back home it doesn't rain like it used to. We have given you our rainy season.'

'And your hot season,' I say.

'India is far too dry now. And when you have no water nothing grows, everything dies.'

'Is it true people get killed for stealing water?'

Mo nods. 'My uncle killed someone. They were stealing the supply to the village. It is allowed to defend your water supply by any means. He was a good man, my uncle, a peaceful man, he changed after that.'

'He was protecting others. Your uncle was a hero.'

'We still have to live with what we do.'

'And we have to do things in order to live.'

Mo offers me some of his curry and I tell him I can't even finish my sandwich. Happiness fills you up as well as giving you a scent like a dog on heat. The rest of the day is busy, parts to order, customers to quote for, stock levels to check. The workshop's busy too and it keeps Malik well away. He only appears at the end of the day, see him barge straight into Kojak's office for an argument. Mo's name gets mentioned and I wander over to stand at the door to earwig but Kojak's air con makes too much noise and I can't hear what they're saying. I give up trying to listen.

Saturday, 4th June 2022

It's been three days and I've heard nothing. I don't know how long I'm supposed to wait, don't know how this shit works. I text her every day, sent heart emojis, rang her twice yesterday. Went to voicemail every time. I didn't leave a message but this morning when I'm getting ready for work I do.

I know it's early, I say, but I'm worried about you so thought I'd call round after work. All the time I talk I'm hoping she'll butt in say she's sorry, she mislaid her phone or say she's sick. She doesn't but as I'm about to walk out the door her name flashes up.

'Hi,' I say.

I want to sound cool, chilled, but my voice bounces all over the place like a fucking puppy.

'Why you ringing at this time of the morning?' Her voice is opposite to bouncy.

'You haven't returned any of my calls, my texts, I thought something had happened to you.'

'Sorry, been a bit busy, with revision and stuff.'

It's like I'm having a conversation with a stranger, like we've never met, never kissed, never had sex. She clears her throat.

'I've got a mad few weeks coming up, extra classes, and I was thinking—'

Her voice is getting smaller and smaller and I have to strain to hear her.

'—it might be good if we had a break. Just for a few weeks, that's

45

all. I need some space right now, got so much to do. Please don't take it the wrong way.'

What other way is there? What other way can I take it?

She says it again. Uses that word. Space. Keeps using it like I don't know what it means, like I don't know what she's saying, like I don't understand it's code for fuck off.

'Don't worry about it,' I say.

'I knew you'd be like this.'

Don't want to talk to her. Don't want to listen to her. The sound of her voice doesn't make me happy anymore. It's like she's ringing me from Mars, it's like all this space has been dumped between us. I end the call, look around the kitchen. It's the same as it was yesterday. Nothing's changed. My world's been up-ended and everything looks exactly the same as it did five minutes ago. I look out the window, look at the sky. Maybe that would be enough space. I should ring her back, say she should try being an astronaut, try floating about in all that emptiness, see how that makes her feel. I should ask her exactly how much space she wants. A universe of space, or something more along the lines of a one bedroom flat.

I've been neglectful. Disloyal. That's why the sun felt so hot yesterday. Temps were supposed to be dropping, stabilising. I don't care what the forecast says, they can't be trusted. They put out what they want. I take a can of coke out the fridge, wrap my hands around it. The cold bleeds into my fingers. I've been neglectful, I need to get back on track, stay loyal to the one that has never let me down. Never betrayed me, yet.

I listen to the number ring out, wait for the answerphone to kick in.

'Car Repair Shop. Please leave message. We get back.'

Kojak's voice is thick, coarse, like the oil from a fucked engine. I tell him in my best coughing voice I won't be in today as I've got a sore throat and temperature. Keep it short and sweet like he does. I end the call, switch my phone to silent and slip it into the side pocket of my rucksack. He won't like the fact I fucked off early yesterday and now I'm fucking off my Saturday morning shift.

I look around, make sure I've packed everything and catch sight of it through the kitchen window. It's fuzzy and blurry, like it's just woken up. I watched him last night. The weatherman. Getting all excited in his short sleeves, talking high thirties and low forties, the whole country lit up with orange sunspots. The Amber Alert continues, but could be upgraded from low to high. That's what he said. We're still going to be hitting the high thirties for the next few days, so keep those weather apps updated for any news and, as always, slap it on, cover up and Stay Sun Safe!

It takes two bus rides to get to the Lea and then it's a good forty-five minutes' walk to the site. Should take two hours max. On the way there I go over everything in my head. That was one of the first things Cadets taught me. The importance of repetition. How you have to go over and over things, again and again, until you don't have to think, until your body just does it, until it's pure reflex.

When I get off at the last stop there's a thin scrape of a cloud. Hasn't a chance against this sun. It's only ten and the heat's already stacking up. Be hairdryer hot soon. I got a proper hat on today, foreign legion style sun hat, protects the neck, the face. I stick my shades on and head for the river. I soon get into a nice steady rhythm. The rucksack isn't too heavy and I'm in good time, so there's no need to rush, can take it slow and steady. The path gets scruffier, more overgrown as I near the site. When the tops of the warehouses come into view I peel off down a side road.

We were visiting a company at the back of this industrial site. Kojak dragged me along as his sidekick. Remember going past in the car, seeing the block of warehouses with the huge skylights. Could imagine it inside when the sun struck, how the light would shine in. We came up again last week. A wholesaler changed hands and Kojak needed to vet the new supplier. Funny how I tried to get out of going, said there was stock to count. He was having none of it. We ended up running late and Kojak bounced the car through the site. We hit a crater in the road, my head hit the roof. Then I looked out the window and saw the end warehouse. Derelict. Padlocked. A great zigzag of a hole in the skylight. Couldn't help but throw a salute.

These places shut down for the weekend, they're for tradespeople, not the general public. When we were up last week I was able to do a full recce. Only spotted two cameras I need to worry about.

As I near, the warehouses come back into view, see them peeking up like a mini mountain range. I imagine the derelict one, the sun pouring through the broken skylight, shining down like one big fuck off spotlight. Can feel it rising. Can feel it filling my chest with helium. Feel so light I could float away, float right up to those fucking peaks, float right in through that fucking skylight.

I stand opposite the site and check my watch. Two minutes to eleven. Bang on. One of the CCTV cameras is at the entrance and the other is positioned halfway down the warehouse block. I can see the one covering the entrance is still facing the same direction it was before, so I'm guessing there's no motion sensor. I approach it from behind, keep out the viewing range and slip past it. I stick close to the buildings as I make my way through the site then I drop down the cut between Thomson Electrics and MGN Spares as I near the warehouses. There's a discarded pallet leaning up against a wall. I pick it up and when I exit, I check left. The second camera is about ten yards away and it's looking straight across at the building opposite it. Won't catch anything at either end of the block.

I look to my right and see the warehouse. It's still derelict, still with a great gaping hole in its roof but it's been gated off by a seven-foot wire security fence. I walk up to the fence, place the pallet on the ground in front of it, take a few steps back and run at it, hard. I slam my feet on to the pallet like a springboard, claw for the top and I'm up and over with hardly a scratch.

The main doors are well and truly locked and someone's used a good-sized padlock and a heavy metal chain. I check out the window. Nailed over with hardboard, whoever's done it hasn't done a very good job, a corner's gone already. Only takes one sharp tug. The nails pop easy, don't even need the knife. No tricks behind either — no grills, no wires — just your bog standard four-paned window. I dig around in the rucksack for the hammer. It's right at the bottom. The glass is gone in seconds. The struts aren't as rotten as they look but they soon give. I try and get rid of as many sharp leftovers as possible before I unzip my hoodie and take it off. I lay it over the busted frame and stick my head inside. It's breathtaking the way the light falls all the way from the roof in shafts.

I lower the rucksack inside and climb in. Pick up a few splinters and a sharp piece of glass draws a long red scratch down my shin. Once I'm inside I allow myself a proper look. The way it streams in, the way it beams down, it's magic. The shape of the broken skylight makes the light fall in folds and there's light on light, making shadows that aren't really shadows. It's like being inside a cathedral. Like opening the very last Christmas present and finding out it's the thing you wanted the most.

The warehouse isn't completely empty, there's some stray bits of packaging lying around – cardboard boxes, tubing, plastic sheeting

– shit like that. I kick what looks like a chunk of tyre. It tumbles across the floor and lands in the middle of the spotlight, like it's waiting for its Star Trek moment. I walk over, step inside and join it. I lift my arms up, wave them about, and the golden light thick with dust, splinters sunshine. I've got my very own glitter dome.

It's starting. The spinning. Can feel it deep down in my guts. Can feel the whirlpool picking up speed, getting stronger and stronger. Me and Mum went on the waltzers once. The fairground guy fancied her, so he spun us so fast all we could do was slam our eyes shut and grab hold of the bar. I remember the faster it got the more the whirlpool spun and then this laugh, this screech of a laugh came out. Dad said it was the fear making me hysterical. It wasn't fear. It was because I didn't want it to stop.

I lie down on the floor and the heat pins me to the ground and I wonder how long I can stay here without moving, without turning my head. Sunlight shines through my eyelids and I see the mushy pinkness of my own blood inside my skin. Feel every hair on my face. Feel prickles of sweat coming out of every pore. They used to torture people like this, tie them to the ground and tape their eyelids open. I try and stick it out but I can't. I have to roll away and the crap on the floor sticks to me. I get up spitting, tasting tar.

I take out a water bottle, drink most of it and pour the rest over my face. Need to get on. Need to focus. I empty the rucksack, line it all up: sugar, small magnifying mirrors, Swiss Army knife, notebook, hammer, tissues, newspapers, tape measure.

With the top screwed on, I cut the bottom off the empty bottle, turn it upside down and make a funnel for the sugar. That way you keep a standard thickness. Got to keep things standard otherwise it isn't a proper test. I'm testing ignition times today. See if double or triple magnification makes any difference. Got three magnifying mirrors. The free-standing kind, the ones you can swivel to get a close up of your face.

Only need to use one of them for the first test. I place it flat in the spotlight and light flares off it straight into my eyes. I sort the bonfires next. I measure the distances out from the mirror and then build a small ignition pile out of tissues, and then a larger one out of newspapers and some of the rubbish lying around. I build them to the standard heights for bonfire one and bonfire two. Then I lay the sugar trail between the bonfires.

When I finish I take off my watch. Best present Mum ever got me. Said it was from them both, her and Dad, but I knew it was all her. Six hundred quid it cost. Sapphire lens, GPS, alarm, timer, stopwatch, sunrise/sunset alerts, electronic compass and a chroma display, which means it's readable at any time, even if the sun is shining. I lay it down next to my notepad, stand the mirror up inside the spotlight, adjust the position. When I'm happy with the angle I start the stopwatch.

The rays soon get to work on the tissues. I watch them discolour, turn that shitty manila colour. Same colour as the bills Dad hid. I found them in a suitcase. Hadn't even opened them, just shoved them under the bed. The tissues ignite in 9.4 seconds and then 3.2 seconds later, the smell of burnt sugar catches my throat. I follow the flames as they burn up the sugar trail. They leave a line of singed goo behind and the sweetness makes me crave toffee. I stamp the flames out as they reach the second bonfire. Don't want that to ignite. Not on the first test.

Test 1 = 25.7 seconds in total

For Test 2, I position a second mirror fifty centimetres outside the spotlight, to double the magnification. As I angle it to lengthen the rays I hear a slow crunching. Tyres. Fucking tyres. Somebody's outside. Somebody's driving around right out-fucking-side. A shadow slides under the door. It moves right to left. It's heading south, that means it'll have to go all the way to the end of the block and come all the way back up the other side, before it does a left and passes the busted window. Should give me enough time.

A familiar whining jerks my head towards the front of the warehouse as I grab the rucksack. Used to practise reverse wheelies near the Red Wreck, got really good at doing them, and whoever's at the wheel sounds as though they've practised them too. The car backs up fast and comes to a halt outside the main doors. By the sound of the engine, it's an old BMW. Definitely not the police or anyone official. I'm guessing a clapped-out part-time security guard, using his own clapped-out security vehicle. I hear a car door open and the grating sound of footsteps. I think about making a run for it, but I'd never get out and over the fencing in time.

'I know someone's in there.'

The voice is gruff, blokey. I'm guessing the only exercise he gets is when he has to get out of his car and go suss something out. I track his steps as he walks towards the window. He's not a fast mover and I make it to the window before he does. If he gets any kind of view inside, he'll see the bonfire and it'll be game over. I stand as tall as I can and puff my chest out to fill the frame with as much of me as possible.

He's as I imagined – square, stocky, fifty something. He's wearing a checked shirt and cowboy hat and as I raise my hands in the air he stares at me from the other side of the wire fence.

'I didn't break in to nick anything, there's nothing here, it's empty,' I say. 'I needed a place to sleep, that's all. Somewhere to get my head down, out of sight of the patrols. You know what they're like, always wanting to keep the streets clean.'

A radio is hooked to his top pocket and a bunch of keys swings from his belt. The sun's shining right into his eyes and he has to angle his head and adjust the brim of his hat to get a better look at me.

'I'm alone, there's no one else here, honest.'

He waves his hand, indicating he wants me to move away from the window. I stay put so he does it again.

This time I do move and I move quick. I jam my hands down onto the busted frame, heave myself up and over. Small pieces of razor-sharp glass dig into my palms as I climb out. Blood trickles from my left hand. It's only a surface cut but I crack on it's a lot worse than it is.

'Mate, I've cut myself,' I say, holding my hand and wincing.

'I'm not your mate,' he says, backing away. 'And don't pull any more stupid stunts like that. You stay right where you are. Don't move. Do not move.'

He unhooks his radio and I shout as hard as I can, hurt my throat from yelling so hard. 'There! Over there! Look!'

He can't stop himself, it's reflex. As he turns to look over his shoulder, I claw my way up the fencing like a cat. He's got a bit of a head start on me, but not much and his body wasn't built for flight mode. As he heads back to his car, I make good ground. It's like a cheetah in its prime chasing an old injured wildebeest. I've got two things he hasn't – youth and fitness. I reach behind me and pull out the hammer that's wedged down the back of my jeans. The first blow is the most important. Needs to be on target, because you never ever get the advantage of surprise again.

It's a decent enough strike, lands just behind the ear, enough to make him stumble. As he does I land another. He goes down, goes face first and the radio skitters across the road.

'All I wanted to do was finish what I'd started,' I say. 'You should have left me alone.'

I hit him again and this time I hear the skull give, hear the bone splinter. I hit him one more time to be sure then turn him over. His eyes are shut and his nose and cheek are bleeding but he's still breathing. I take hold of his jaw, move his head from side to side. The muscles are slack. He's not going to be waking up any time soon. When I let go, his head rolls to one side and blood, black as diesel oil, crawls out of his ear. I stand up and shove the hammer back inside my waistband. He's making the kind of snoring noises you get with a cold. I pick up his cowboy hat and place it over his face.

Never seen so many keys on one bunch. Takes me a while to work out which one opens the padlock on the fencing. The main warehouse doors are easier. It's an old-style lock with a monster of a key. I sit him up and then I slide my hand underneath his armpits and then wrap my arms around his chest. He's wearing cowboy boots to match his hat and they scrape along the road as I drag him. A set of chalky tramlines follows us all the way into the warehouse.

I need all my strength to pull his body along the floor of the warehouse and I have to do it in short bursts. I finally lay him down next to the unlit bonfire and sit beside him, take a minute to get my breath and wipe the sweat from my face. I take off my hat and my whole head feels wet, like if I've been out in the rain. Once I've steadied my breathing I get up and walk over to the column of light. It's shining brighter, and the dust is even more glittery. When I step inside the heat feels raw on my skin.

I tilt my head and look up at the broken skylight. I'm wearing heavy-duty sunglasses and using my hands to shade my eyes but the sunlight still hurts.

'I feel your anger and I hear your call,' I say. 'And I am ready.'

It doesn't take long to rebuild the bonfire on top of him. He's not snoring anymore, his breathing is shallow, fast. I draw two sun symbols on the ground with the sugar. One at his head, the other at his feet. It feels as if I've been called here, to this place, to this moment. And so was he.

My notebook lies open and face down near the remains of the first bonfire. Had to kick it out of the way when I dragged him inside. I pick it up find the page and read aloud.

I offer up this sacrifice
In honour and respect

Without you there is only darkness
You are the power and the light
The almighty giver of life
From the Sun God we came
To the Sun God we return

I use the sugar to draw a circle around his body and the symbols, and as I do I repeat the last four lines. *You are the power and the light. The almighty giver of life. From the Sun God we came. To the Sun God we return.*

The words become a rhythm and the rhythm becomes a beat. I shut my eyes, let my feet move in time and then my body joins in. All I need to do is trust and let go. Not sure how long I dance for but when I stop I can feel the energy inside me. I stretch my hands out in front of me. Not a sign, not a hint. Completely steady. There's no crazy rush, I'm in total control and there's no doubt, no fear.

I stare at the small bonfire on top of the guard's belly. It's still, silent. No hint of any movement. I pick up one of the mirrors, hold it near his mouth. Nothing. No sign of breath.

The Mayans believed death was a phase. It was not an ending, it was merely a change. The spirit, the soul, would continue to exist but in a different form. Sacrifice was the unleashing and sending of the soul back to the giver.

From the Sun God we came
To the Sun God we return

I focus the last mirror. Use the sharp edge of my knife, whip it across the base of my thumb. Blood oozes. I let it well, then shake my hand over the body. Bright drops fall and spot the kindling. I stand back. The sun's rays soon ignite the bonfire. I watch the flames spread out, climb higher. I watch them reach up, stretch as high they can, then settle back down. The flames spread along his clothes. The smell of scorching, hair singeing, gives way to another smell. I cover my face, pack my things quickly and leave.

Monday, 6th June 2022

Hear Malik before I see him. He's at the counter cackling because my face is the colour of a baboon's arse. I walked all the way home on one of the hottest days ever. Couldn't chance public transport, didn't want any CCTV evidence and they'd have questioned me being out during a High Amber Alert. Tried to keep to the back roads to dodge the Sun Patrols to avoid the same questioning. There was no air, just heat. Had to really pace myself. Tried to stay in the shade as much as possible but I couldn't avoid it completely.

Stayed in my room all Sunday. Said I was sick. If I held my hands near my face could feel the heat radiating off it. Was lying there like that when Celine came in. She pretended she was checking if I was OK but all she wanted to do was tell me she was getting a new phone off Mum for her birthday. I told her to fuck off and she got the message.

I was angry anyway, not because of the sunburn but because of the watch. It was a present from Mum. She gave it to me at my passing out parade. I remember taking it off to do the timings and I thought I'd picked everything up. It must have fell out the rucksack when I climbed back out. That was careless. Too careless.

I head to the sink in the backroom. The warm water coming out the cold tap doesn't make a great job of cooling my face.

'If the Skin Doctors see you, you is proper fucked, man.' Malik says. 'You need to take more care. Your white skin, it doesn't tan very well, does it?'

The jangle of the doorbell rescues me. Can tell by the wheezing it's Kojak, such an effort to move that gut of his. Malik hears him too and scuttles back into the yard. I wipe my face with a scummy teacloth while I try and get an excuse together.

'These mothers. They owe me.'

Kojak takes my hand and shoves a bunch of invoices into it. I wait for him to kick off, to give out about me ringing in sick with a sore throat and then turning up with third degree burns, but he just gives me the paperwork and walks off. He says he'll be back by lunchtime then disappears off on another of his errands. I spend the morning ringing suppliers, chasing payments. There's a lot of people owe him. Some invoices go back to the beginning of the year. By twelve I need a breather from my debt-collecting duties, so I take an early for lunch.

I've nearly finished when Malik comes and joins me. He doesn't say anything. Sits at the table reading a paper. He holds it up in front of him to blank me out and I'm quite happy to be blanked out.

A photo takes up the whole of the front page. Something big is ablaze but I can't make out what. I read the headline underneath: *WAREHOUSE FIRE EAST LONDON.*

I try and lean forward, get a better look. There's another, smaller heading: *Art Worth Millions Destroyed By Fire.* Need to see whereabouts in east London but can't because my eyes won't stay put. They dart about like trapped mice. I lean as far forward as I can and then I see it.

LEYTON.

There's a tingle in my left shoulder blade. I want to read on but Malik snatches the paper away. He stares at me as he folds it in half and tucks it under his arm.

'Get your own fucking paper,' he says. I wait until he disappears then I do the same. I walk out past reception, through the door, across the road and into the newsagents.

There's a natty little map on page two. Some clever bastard's done an exact replica of the Lea Valley Industrial site. The warehouses are drawn in black dotted lines. They do that when something doesn't exist anymore.

They've even drawn the river. It's a skinny squiggle in the right-hand corner.

Doesn't seem real. Like something you'd find in a comic, like a map of Treasure Island. 'X' marks the spot. 'X' marks the bonfire.

There's a bee, angry as fuck, trapped inside my head. Can hardly concentrate for the buzzing. Says the fire started between one and 2pm. The buzzing noise is so loud I can't think straight. They've got it as starting in the same warehouse I was in but they're saying it was full of electrical stuff. They've got that wrong too, it was empty, it was fucking empty. I look to see if there's anything about how it started. There's too much to read. Pages and pages of it. Fucking pages. I smack my forehead and the bee kicks off again.

I have to stay focused. I have to get through the afternoon. I have to think about all the skills I learnt when we did the Three Peaks trials after days of training and little food. Nights of hardly sleeping. I remember the main thing is to try and keep out the bad thoughts. The ones that want to invade, cloud your judgement, sabotage. When you're under stress, keep to the present. If you can't you'll never succeed. You'll never get through it. I don't check the news updates. I switch off my phone. I keep my head down. I chase the invoices and I make it to hometime.

Mum's working late, so I'm doing dinner. Egg, sausage, beans. Celine lays the table. We eat, don't talk, she knows I'm not in the mood. Make sure I finish first so I can hog the sofa. I sit there flicking through the channels. They're showing the same image that was in the paper, the fire in full flow. As the camera pans back I see there's an army of firemen trying to put it out. They haven't got a fucking hope, it's like pissing into hell.

I flick on, hit a live report. A lone fireman in a field of ash is waving a rag in the air like he's surrendering, like he's the last man standing. There's a voiceover saying the tatty bit of material in his hand is all that's left of the artwork that was stored in one of the warehouses. A few burnt-out frames are the only signs the warehouses existed and in the middle there's just a dirty grey hole, like a meteor hit.

Celine shoves my feet on the floor and flumps down next to me. She kicks off her shoes and draws her knees up under her chin and the next thing I know some glinty rap star's singing and eyeballing me at the same time. I grab the remote back. They're showing the fire again. In amongst it all you can make out the blackened frames of the warehouses. Barbequed ribs. Barbequed fucking ribs.

'Since when did you get so interested in the news?' Celine asks. She's still in her uniform, her hair scraped back into a tight ponytail. The summer's brought her freckles out, smeared them across her cheekbones like glitter. Just as I'm thinking how young they make her look she rips her hairband out, shakes her head. She's only fourteen but she's got this shape, like a proper woman. It's all there. The plain shirt and school tie can't hide it, not with all that thick hair spilling over her shoulders.

'You should keep it tied back.'

'What?'

'Your hair, you should keep it tied back,' I say.

'Like I care what you think.'

She unwraps her knees, slips down the sofa as if she's about to slide off, then drums her fingers on her belly. 'You actually watching this?'

They keep showing the same image, sheets of flames tearing through the warehouses. I rewind the bit where the timber gives way, watch the shower of sparks fall in slow motion. It's like when I put my head through the window, saw the light pouring in. It's like that but a hundred, a thousand times better.

'Why you watching this? It's boring.'

'We were talking about it at work.'

'Who?'

'Me and a mate.'

She turns to look at me. 'You got mates?'

I tell her to fuck off. She sucks at her teeth and I say it again. It's the same voice Dad used with Mum when he'd had enough. It works, it sends her away but before she goes she makes a point of standing right in front of me, so I have to move to see the TV.

'Oh,' she says with a mock yawn. 'Forgot. Someone called for you earlier.'

'Someone?'

'Some bloke.'

'What bloke?'

She doesn't reply so I have to repeat it.

'Dunno,' she says lazily. 'A bloke.'

'What did he want?'

'You. He wanted Luke Spargo.'

She announces my name like I've won something. She thinks she's so clever, sitting there beside me on the sofa all that time, knowing she had something to tell me, knowing it would wind me up. I keep my eyes fixed on the TV and she gets the message and goes upstairs.

When I hear the bass coming through the ceiling I slide the

paper out from under the sofa. Soon as I open it I hear Mum's key twist in the door. I pass her in the hallway, she's laden down with bags. She wants me to help but I'm up the stairs before she finishes the sentence. I shut the door behind me, switch the radio on, whack up the volume and lie back on the bed.

Read every word. The bits I like, I read out loud to myself in a voice that a reporter might use.

It is thought the fire is likely to have started in a derelict warehouse and spread throughout the rest of the block. Currently there is no confirmation as to whether arson is suspected or whether the searing temperatures on the day alone contributed. The Fire Service is already overstretched and the public are urged to remain vigilant and to follow government advice. A High Amber Alert had been issued for that day and the Emergency Services have repeated their call for vigilance regarding the use of lit flames and keeping of fuel and solvents and the ban on barbeques and outside fires is unlikely to be lifted during the foreseeable future.

I really like how they've used the word 'likely' at the beginning and 'unlikely' at the end. That's neat. I sit up, spread the newspaper out over the bed and take my knife out of my bedside drawer. This version has loads of extras – screwdriver, wire stripper, corkscrew, tweezers, can opener – even a fucking toothpick. It's beautiful – the shiny metal spilling out of the red lacquer. Snap everything shut apart from my favourite. The scissors do a neat job. Doesn't take long before the duvet's covered in cuttings. All this writing, all these pictures, all because of me. Never felt like this when the moors went up. That only got a paragraph in the local paper. Definitely didn't make the news. I knew then the summers were getting dryer. Knew then the sun was getting stronger. The grass was dry as fuck. Panicked at first. Wasn't meaning to burn such a big hole in the hills but the fire wouldn't stop, kept spreading. Left behind this scorched patchwork. You could see it for miles. The paper gave it a name, called it 'The Fallen Angel of the North'. It did look like it had wings. I was so mad it didn't get on TV. They didn't want anyone suggesting the weather played any part. There were so many fires back then and not enough firefighters. At least they've put that right.

'Luke.'

All those headlines.

'Luke!' Mum shouts my name again. 'Somebody's at the door!'

I scoop up the clippings, shove them under the bed and dust

down my jeans as I close the bedroom door behind me. Celine's at the top of the stairs.

'Must be one of your so-called *mates*.'

When she says *mates*, she makes air quotes with her fingers. Bunny ears, as she calls them. I push past her.

'Loser,' she whispers again.

This time I'm ready. Ready for whoever, whatever. She's got it so wrong. I'm not a loser. I'm not that kid who left school with one poxy qualification, who ended up working in a poxy garage on minimum poxy wage. I'm Luke Spargo. Sun worshipper. Fire Starter. Saviour. Stick that in your fucking pipe.

Kojak's on the path, his BMW parked up by the kerb. Engine running, driver door open. He chucks a bunch of keys at me, shouts over his shoulder as he walks back to his car.

'Open up in morning. I have meeting. Be back later.'

He prises himself into the seat and gives me one last instruction. 'Remember, you in charge. Don't take any shit from anyone.'

As he pulls away I finger the keys, slip them into my pocket.

Tuesday, 7th June 2022

Malik does a double take when he sees me. It's only eight o'clock and I'm not usually in until half past. I do the same because he's got on a pair of smart blue shorts and a smart white shirt. Never comes to work in his best.

'Mo's made a start on the Astra already,' I say, looking up from the job book.

Hear the tap of his shoes. Not wearing his usual trainers either. He stands at the counter and swivels the job book to face him.

'Why you swapping stuff around?'

'That Volvo needs an MOT, it'll need more work. Makes sense to start on the other first.'

'Fat Boy likes us to get the easy shit out the way first.'

I tell him Kojak's out all day and I'm in charge.

'So unless you want to work through your breaks, you better get changed and start back to work.'

He shoves his hands in the pockets of his shorts and takes his time with the return.

'Did you take my paper?'

I keep my head down. Keep my eyes fixed on today's entries.

'Only I saw you with it yesterday.'

I run my finger down the page.

'Lukey Boy gone deaf all of a sudden?'

I mutter something about having seen Mo with it and he slaps his hands down hard on the counter and it makes me jump.

63

'Now I know you're winding me up.'

He cracks his knuckles and walks off howling. The fact I think Mo would have taken his paper is hilarious. He teases Mo about it all morning. I could stop it but him giving his brother grief stops him giving me grief.

Want an early lunch. Need to listen to the radio. Need to see if they're still talking about the fire. The phone rings as I'm about to take my break. It's Irish. He wants to know when he can book in his fleet of taxis. It's the third time he's rang this morning. Kojak's told me not to book them in, says he needs to speak to Irish about it but he won't speak to him about anything. He won't speak to him at all. Keeps avoiding him and Irish keeps hassling me.

'Sorry, Kojak's not around. I don't think he'll be back until tomorrow. All I can suggest is to ring his mobile.'

'I already did. You tell him, soon as you see him, you tell him Irish needs a word. Tell him I don't like being messed about.'

'I will,' I say.

'Make sure you do and make sure you tell him that if he doesn't get in touch by noon tomorrow, the fucking deal's off.'

He hangs up and I go out and check on the Astra. It's jacked up in the yard. Mo's underneath it. Recognise the cheap trainers. I kick his feet and he slides into view like a pop tart.

'You nearly done?'

'Yes, boss.'

Mo's never moans, just does the work. I tell him he can break early for lunch.

'OK, boss,' he says.

Boss. I stick my hands in my pockets, look around me. It's not much of a garage, holds six cars max, but today it's mine and it feels good. I like it. I like being in charge. I like having someone call me boss. I ask where Malik is.

'He's already gone for lunch,' he says.

It's only just gone twelve; we don't normally break until half past. He wouldn't do this if Kojak was here.

'Did he say where he was going?'

Mo shakes his head. 'It will be OK. I can finish his jobs. Need to keep boss happy.'

Mo doesn't want to break for lunch, keeps on working. I'm boss for the day, I may as well go and check out the boss's office, make a few calls. I take the garage keys from their peg at reception. Kojak's office is a sweatbox of a room and it's a dump. Rickety wooden desk and chair, beat-up metal filing cabinet. No windows, airless, tiny, shit air con. It's like a fucking cell.

I pull the door to, switch on the air con and the desk fan. He's got a mini calendar sellotaped to his desk, shows the year at a glance. I count backwards from the twenty-first to today's date. Fourteen days. Two weeks today, it will be the summer solstice. There'll be people gathered everywhere to celebrate the longest day. But in fourteen days' time there might be no more days. If the sun hasn't been honoured, if the sun hasn't been respected, pacified, it will be a date that won't be a celebration of light, only darkness.

I sit down behind the desk, open the desk drawer. Broken pencil, two biros, three rubber bands, a few odd staples, no stapler. I lean back, put my hands behind my head and my feet up on the desk.

I pick up the phone and tip back in the chair to rest against the wall behind me.

'Hey, Malik, boss here,' I say, in as good a Kojak accent as I can. 'I think I work you too hard so take a break. Take a shit-cat. In fact, take a big break you lazy piece of cat shit. You fired, you lazy fuck. You hear me. Fired.'

I lean forward, slam the phone down and the chair skids down the wall. I fling my arms out to the side, grab hold of the filing cabinet to steady myself. The cabinet feels heavy, full. I get up, tug at the top drawer. It doesn't budge. I look for a key amongst the bunch that might open it. A small square-headed silver one. Don't find one. I try the filing cabinet drawer again, give it a good yank. For a second, I think it's going to give, sticks its lip out, lets me see inside. Paperwork – receipts, invoices.

I try again but the cabinet rocks backwards and forwards and all I end up doing is dislodging the stack of old car magazines lying on top of it. They fall and as I bend down to pick them up I see a white envelope on the floor. It's not sealed and the flap has fallen open. Two head-and-shoulder shots of a girl. Passport style. Young, dark, thick black eyebrows like Kojak. He's never mentioned a daughter, only ever talked about his sons. I turn the photos over. There's a signature scribbled on the back, printed out in small neat capitals underneath. RUPINDA JA. The phone rings and I shove the photos back inside the envelope, slip the envelope inside the magazine and pile them all on top of the cabinet.

The phone stops by the time I reach it. It'll only be Irish again.

I walk over to the windowsill, turn the apple then look out the window. Mo's got his head stuck under the bonnet of a car. Sleeves rolled up, arms elbow deep, he's got the same look of concentration you see in those medical documentaries. The ones where a surgeon is up to their armpits inside a patient. Always looks like they've got their hands stuck in a huge pile of tripe but then they start describing it. Bit by fucking bit. Every slippy-slidey piece. They know exactly what it is, what it does and where it goes. Just like Mo.

I go out and tell him he's done good. 'I'll make sure I tell Kojak,' I say.

He looks pleased. I ask him for Malik's number. He gives it to me and I ring it.

'I can finish jobs. Don't worry, I can work fast, no problem.'

Malik doesn't answer. 'Did he tell you where he was going?'

Mo shakes his head and says sorry. Malik's done it on purpose because Kojak's left me in charge. He wants me to fail, wants me to fall face down into the shit.

I tell him his brother's a twat. Mo repeats it. It's the first time I've ever heard him swear.

'Twat. Twat. Twat.'

The way he says it. Slow, definite, it's hilarious.

'Got your funny bone switched on today, Mo.'

I hold my hand up ready for a high five but Mo looks straight past me. Malik's standing on the back step, big cheesy grin on his face.

'Sorry to interrupt, guys.'

There's someone standing at the side of him, I can see a shadow.

'Meet Scarlet,' Malik says.

A girl, tall, long red hair straight as sheet metal, comes to stand beside him. She's got on a huge sun hat and it nearly pokes Malik's eye out. Scarlet smiles and shifts her weight and her tits do a little jiggle under the dress she's got on. She's not wearing a bra and her nipples are pencil points.

'No need to stare, Lukey Boy, but in case you're wondering they're real, nothing fake going on here.'

Malik squeezes Scarlet's right breast and as he does she looks at me and blows me a kiss. It's a green light for my dick. I have no fucking control.

'You got a fan there, Lukey Boy,' Malik says.

Scarlet yanks his hand away. 'You do that again and I'll bite your nuts off.'

I don't know if she's talking to me or Malik.

'Told you she was feisty.'

Malik grins and so does Scarlet, because I'm going as red as her fucking name, red as the fucking Peugeot Malik was supposed to be working on. I want to ask him where he's been, what he's playing at, tell him lunchtime finished an hour ago, but I don't. I take a litre bottle of water out of the fridge and stand in front of the open door, let the cold air comfort me.

A few minutes later I see Scarlet walk past the front window. She looks in, sees me sitting at reception and waves. I get up, press my face to the glass, watch her walk down the street. She looks nicer on her own.

As a punishment, I take the radio. Walk straight into the workshop and lift it down from the ledge.

'I don't want to hear anything other than you doing work,' I say.

I put the radio under the counter at reception. Tune into a news station, keep the volume down low. I could listen to the news on my phone but Kojak's anal about wearing headphones. Gives out wrong impression, it's about customer, not you.

The reporter has got her good news voice on. UK temperatures have dropped by four degrees since Sunday and no current alerts are in place. She is so fucking happy that she nearly forgets to remind us of the need to still be mindful. Fucking mindful? Respectful. That's the word she needs. Her good news voice disappears as she announces there is live breaking news.

We are hearing unconfirmed reports of a missing person. A guard believed to have been at the site is still unaccounted for.

I lift the radio to my ear. They haven't mentioned the location. I don't think I could have missed it because it cut straight to it.

A team of investigators continue to search through the remains. We will update you as soon as any further details become available.

That's it. Half a story. Fucking useless. How can you flash up breaking news and only give half a story?

'We supposed to eat our lunch in that room with your rancid fruit still on the windowsill.'

I switch off the radio, think about picking it up and smashing it into Malik's face.

'It's definitely a health and safety issue, if someone walked in today they could shut this place down.'

I imagine him at the end of a sugar trail, a bonfire built around him. He'd make a great Guy Fawkes in his oil-soaked overalls. No need for an accelerant. Sometimes all you have to do is wait and the way forward will present itself.

'There's a mix on that Peugeot I'm working on, not one tyre the same,' he says. 'You seen the manual anywhere?'

'It's in Kojak's office,' I say.

As soon as he steps inside, I grab the keys and pull the door to. I have to be quick but I manage to lock the door before he realises.

'Come on, open the door. I got work to do, remember.'

He doesn't hold back. Bangs his fist on the door, kicks it.

'You planning on keeping me in here all day? You think Mo can do it all on his own? That'll really impress Kojak, if we fall behind. You know he doesn't like leftovers.'

'Thought you might want a break, seeing how hard you hard you been working. Sit back and enjoy, I would.'

He switches the air con on. Hear the dodgy motor wind itself up. Any luck it'll break down. I listen to him shouting the odds as I neck a drink from the bottle. The water's not icy anymore but I only want to quench my thirst. Won't be long before Malik gets thirsty, stuck inside that sweat box, even with the air con and the fan on. Be dead in less than two days without water now. Less for very young and the very elderly and if you're stuck inside a car or a coffin sized room, it's probably hours. Always best to carry water with you. They should stick that on their Mindful Sun Safe mantra.

I sit doodling at the back of the job book. Draw a mini Malik, put him on the windowsill next to a row of apples. I wonder what would last longest. I think about turning him each day, him ripening, him festering. The Mayans shrunk heads as part of sun worship, so why not whole bodies.

When I finish drinking the litre bottle of water, I tip-toe over, put my ear to the office door. I'm wondering whether the fact he's gone quiet is because he's baiting me into opening the door, or whether he's had enough, when Malik's fist comes down hard the other side of the door. He shouts for Mo. Asks him for help. Different now, isn't it, you're not the strong one anymore, Malik, you're not the cocky brother anymore. Malik hits the door so hard the frame shakes and then he calms down, goes quiet again.

I listen to the radio but there's no more news. Malik's been in there for nearly an hour and he's been silent for the last twenty minutes. He's probably curled up under the air con having a nap, enjoying the fact that I'm stopping him working, and I am. If we fall behind Kojak won't be too pleased.

I get ready for Malik to lunge at me when I push the door open, but he doesn't. I push it open somewhere and peer in. Malik's sat in the middle of the floor in his boxers and work boots. His overalls folded neatly beside him.

'You're doing overtime tonight,' I say.

He picks up his clothes and stands up.

'This isn't over,' he whispers as he walks by.

It's five to five when Kojak shows. He dumps a carrier bag of files down on the counter and asks how things have been.

'Jobs all done?'

'Nearly,' I say. 'Malik had to nip out at lunchtime to take his mother to a hospital appointment, so we're a bit behind.'

'What hospital?'

I say I don't know.

'How behind are we?'

'Two more jobs to get through but Malik's offered to work late.'

'I give you chance and what you do? You repay me with cheap excuse and jobs not finished.'

He pushes the job book towards me. 'One, two, three. Three jobs, not two, three. You can't even count.'

'Like I said, Malik can stay back and—'

Kojak sucks in a deep breath and pushes his belly out so much the buttons on his shirt strain.

'Please, if I want fairy tale I'll ask for one.'

'Mo's offered to stay behind and I will as well. I'll make sure everything gets finished,' I say.

'I think you already done enough.'

'You had a few messages and Irish rang again, it sounded like it was urgent.'

Kojak lowers his head, moves it slowly left to right like a bull sizing up a target. 'Not easy is it, being manager? My fault, you're not ready yet, maybe you never be ready, maybe you need more time. Who knows? Now go home, you look shit.'

I roll up my sleeves when I step outside. Feel the hot kiss on my skin. Fierce as Scarlet's hair. Fierce as the thought that won't go away.

Tuesday, 7th June 2022

I pick up a newspaper on the way home. The fire has been relegated to page four but they've put some words in a box, to make it look newsworthy.

A London Fire Brigade spokesman has declined to comment on the cause, or origin, of the fire but confirms investigations are ongoing.

Yesterday they said the fire was likely due to an electrical fault or the result of the unusual high temperatures. Now it's being treated as suspicious. I'm not worried though. As soon as a bigger disaster pops up this won't be news anymore. They're not really investigating it anyway, just want to give the impression they are. I cut out the article, put it in the box file with the others. The hills. The school. The house. I've kept them all. Kept everything. Hard copy, digital, hidden server. I should get rid of this file, but I like looking at the cuttings, like holding them, like wondering who else has read them. Soon as they stop publishing this latest one, I'll bin the lot.

Mum shouts me down for tea. Her and Celine are sitting next to each other on the sofa, watching a game show, chicken salads balanced on their knees.

As I walk by, Mum tells me Dad won't be coming for Celine's birthday, after all. He's away in Scotland with work. She expects me to thank her, give her a high five, show her how grateful I am but I don't comment. I tell her I'm eating my tea upstairs.

'Don't make a mess,' Mum says.

'The only one making a mess is you, Mum,' I say, as I walk up the stairs. 'You're the one who's let him back in, not me.'

The salad's good. Mum's lemon garlic dressing is spot on tonight. I eat it as I go through my news popups. First one is a good news one. Tomorrow water bottles will be available at all local tube stations free of charge. About time, they've been saying that for weeks. They give the usual tips on how to keep cool at night – no hot meals or hot drinks after six, cold showers before bed, freeze bedsheets, fill hot water bottles with iced water and DRINK. DRINK WATER. DRINK PLENTY OF WATER. No matter how many times they tell people to drink enough water they still won't, and big writing won't make any difference.

I find one about the warehouse. There's a video of the fire. The commentary is being delivered with a fake transatlantic accent.

'It's now looking like the fire was not accidental but deliberate. Any person or persons in the vicinity are encouraged to come forward, as is anyone with information on the whereabouts of the missing guard.

'The remains of a burnt-out car have been found nearby and speculation is rising that this may have been a premeditated arson attack. The Police Commissioner and the Chief Inspector of Fire Services have reiterated that this kind of crime will not be tolerated. The Prime Minister, in an unprecedented move, has stepped in to offer any necessary resources. Firestarters will not be tolerated is the message coming from government.'

They still haven't publicly identified the guard. Sometimes they withhold information to flush out imposters and sometimes they just don't know. Cat and mouse. Mouse and cat.

Lastly, I check the readings. It's more good news. It is true, temps are on the way down and are predicted to continue to fall over the coming week. No restrictions, no alerts.

He's done all this. The missing guard. This is down to him. His life has saved us all. Who could have predicted today would bring such good news? The sun isn't going to die and Dad isn't coming down.

I raise my hands above my head and pump the air with my fists. Can't stay seated, have to get up, have to run downstairs and tell Mum and Celine. Have to tell them the danger has passed, that everything will go back to normal and it's all down to me. I'm at the top of the stairs hyperventilating. I need to bring it right down, my breathing, my mood, because I know what they'll do. They'll pass that look between them, as if I've announced I'm Elvis back from the dead, Jesus reborn. I am a kind of saviour though. Their fucking saviour.

Mum's bedroom door is ajar and light splashes onto the landing. It's a soft, pale light. Nothing harsh about it at all. Nothing punishing.

I am grateful for the sunrise of today
The sunrise of tomorrow
And for each morrow after
You are the giver of light and of life
Without you we are nothing

'Why are you sat in the middle of the landing?'

Celine's behind me, wants me to move. I tell her I'm praying.

'Well can you do it elsewhere, I need to get past.'

As she squeezes by me I grab her ankle.

'Stop being a prick,' she says.

'Say please.'

She kicks out her foot and I hold on to it tigher, lift it higher.

'Let go of me, you crazy fuck!'

'That's not a very nice thing to say, after everything I've done for you, Celine. I do forgive you though, you need to know that. Actually, I need to thank you, it's made me what I am. Forgiving Dad, that's a bit harder, but it will come.'

I let go and she stumbles into her room. Before she shuts the door she tells me to stay away from her. 'That's all I want. For you to keep away.'

It's one of those humid sticky nights and I'm running too fast already. Haven't even reached the bridge. Barely got into the park. I'll have drained my water bottle by the time I reach the hill. I jog over the low bridge, pass the kids' play area and take on the steep rise. At the top I take a breather, look out at the sprawl that is northwest London. Wembley with its boring arc is usually the only thing that attracts any attention, the rest are just mismatched shapes. Not so tonight. The setting sun has worked its alchemy. The two concrete tower blocks that stand side by side like abandoned twins have been turned into bars of pure gold. Pure shimmering, pure shining, twenty-four fucking carat fucking gold.

If that's not a blessing, if that's not a sign, I don't know what is. All I need is for Fee to get back in touch, but I don't want to appear too greedy. That is the downfall that brought us here. If we don't respect what we have, show attention to that which has value, we deserve not to have anything.

It's nearly nine, they'll be shutting the park soon. I jog down the other side of the hill. Pass the car park, tennis courts, loner on a bench. Something about the scummy trainers, the t-shirt, that makes me stop. I walk over, tap Mo on the shoulder. Slumped forward, head in hands, he jumps to his feet like a jack-in-the-box.

'Sorry, sorry, so sorry.'

I wait for him to recognise me but he just keeps squeezing his eyes shut and saying sorry. Won't stop. I take hold of his shoulders.

'Mo, it's me, Luke. Luke from work, from the garage.'

He rolls his head from side to side and his hair is stuck out at odd angles. If I didn't know him better I'd swear he'd been drinking. I shake him and all he does is laugh. I help him to sit back down on the bench and sit down next to him. He's making me nervous because I've never seen him like this before.

'What's up?' I say and he leans forward and starts to rock.

'I can't go back. I can't. I can't go back. Please you speak to them, tell them I am good worker. I am no trouble. Please you tell them, they will listen to you.'

His eyes are red and sore and his bottom lip's doing that quivering, shivering thing, like a kid about to wet himself.

'You're not making any sense, Mo.'

I offer him some water and for a second, I think he's saying 'please' again. But when he repeats I hear it right.

'Police, they will come back. You need to tell them.'

His bottom lip stops quivering, starts dancing, and then he breaks down. Howls like a baby.

'Come back where, Mo? To the garage?'

He nods and I ask him more questions but he's too busy crying and too busy rocking. I lean forward, speak right into his ear.

'Did the police want to speak to me?'

I speak clearly and slowly so he'll understand but Mo won't talk anymore. I grab his Arsenal shirt, use it to drag him to his feet.

'Please, you tell them. You say how good worker I am—'

I twist his shirt around my fists, lift him almost off the ground. He's as limp as a dead kitten.

'Mo, did they want to talk to me?'

I say it loud, but it's like he's gone deaf so I shout it.

'Mo, did the police ask for me? *Did they fucking ask for me?*'

A small crowd has gathered. I let go of Mo's shirt. It's all scrunched and creased where I've gripped it. Mo sinks to his knees and grasps my hands. Holds on to me, begging, crying. His wet snotty lips kissing, sticking to my fingers. I rip my hands away, wipe them on his shirt and leave him there.

Pick up speed as I run back down the hill. A woman is walking a Jack Russell at the bottom. It jiggles along beside her. She pulls at the lead just in time. I pump my arms in time with my legs, beat out the rhythm on the ground.

Wednesday, 8th June 2022

If there was a superhero trait I could pick, it would be teleportation. To be able to go anywhere, at any time, be with someone whenever, wherever, would be the best. Even if they couldn't see you, even if they didn't know you were there, it wouldn't matter. Be enough to be near, be enough to see just the back of them.

Last night in bed, every time I thought about her, every time I got excited, Mo would pop up with that pathetic face. And then all I could think about was the police, and all the good feeling would go, and the shit feeling would press down on me. Thought about not going in. Thought about throwing a sickie, but that would make me look too guilty. Suspects that go missing always look bad and it's not like I haven't got an alibi. If they ask if I've been to the warehouse, I'll tell them the truth. No need to lie. They can wire me up to one of those machines, no sweat. If they found the watch I'll say that's when it went missing, when I went up to the site with Kojak on the visit before. That's airtight as a cat's arse, that alibi. I made a note of our visit in the job book. Can give them the date, time and the name of the supplier.

On the way to work I wonder if they'll be there, lying in wait, but as I near the garage there's no obvious sign, no cop car parked up. I push open the door, try not to jangle the doorbell too much. Kojak's behind the counter, he looks up as I walk towards him.

'Mo called in sick. You need to make sure his lazy fuck of a brother does some work.'

I say OK and Kojak gestures towards his office. Of course, they'll be in there waiting. They'll have been here since we opened.

The office is empty.

'Please, sit.'

Kojak squeezes past the filing cabinet and sits down at his desk. He lowers himself into his chair and I sit down opposite him.

'How long you been working here?' he asks, resting his elbows on the table. Kojak's chair is wooden and every time he moves it creaks.

'Could I have a drink first please?'

Kojak pours me a glass of water from the water jug on his desk. He passes it to me and I notice his hands are twice the size of mine. Everything about him is big, apart from his height.

He watches me take a drink, waiting for my answer.

'Nearly two years.'

He leans back, and the chair creaks louder.

'Happy?'

I nod and his mouth makes a crooked half smile, like the smile of someone who's had a stroke or been to the dentist.

'I'm happy too,' he says.

His smile is odd but not as odd as the look on his face. I sit up in the chair, plant both feet on the ground.

'You're a good worker, one of the best I've had. Not everyone works as hard as you.'

He taps the table a few times and we sit in silence. I realise he hasn't switched the air con on and the warmth suddenly hits me.

'I like you, Luke. You are a good boy.'

He leans across the table and I see his eyes are spinning like fucking planets and I wonder if he's trying to hypnotise me. I clear my throat and go to pour myself another drink but he shoots out his hand and stops me.

'Was thinking maybe time you got a reward. Would you like that?'

He keeps a grip on my hand and I'm wishing that it was the police that were waiting for me because I would know what they wanted, I would know what they're up to.

'What, you don't want better job, better money, you don't want promotion?' He throws his hands in the air. 'You want to be like Malik, you want to be like Lazy Fuck?'

I try to tell him I don't want to be like Malik, that promotion would be great but my mouth won't work properly. It's so dry all I can do is mumble. He shakes his head and I take another drink of water and I go over-the-top grateful.

'No, no, that would be great, I'd love to have a promotion. It's just come as a bit of a shock, that's all. I wasn't expecting it, because of the mess I made the other day when you left me in charge. I kind of ballsed it up and I'm so grateful you haven't held that against me because—'

'What about I make you Financial Director? Give you extra five thousand a year.' He slams his fist down on the desk. 'What you say?'

I don't know what to say and he thinks I'm pausing for effect.

'OK, what about I backdate to April and give you advance?'

He scratches his head. There is not one single hair on it. It's as smooth and shiny as a bowling ball. But he has plenty of hair, just not on his head.

'OK, maybe this will help.'

He plucks a roll of notes from his shirt pocket, peels four away and pushes them across the desk to me. Fifties. He's giving me four fifty-pound notes. Two hundred quid. Two hundred fucking quid. Never seen a fifty before. Good colour. I like red. Like it a lot more now. Soon as I reach out to take one he slams his hand down on mine.

'First, I need you to do something.'

The sleazy look's gone completely. He's in pure bartering mode.

I'm at the desk sorting through job sheets when the police arrive. Kojak was expecting them at ten and he isn't here, because they're three hours late. He did wait two hours before he kicked off. I got out of him that it's the garage they're interested in. The accounts, that's all. Nothing to do with me, nothing to do with the fire. Nothing to do with Mo.

There's two of them. Man cop. Woman cop. Both in regulation white shirts and navy shorts, but that's all they've got in common. He's tall, lanky; she's short, square. They've both got coppers' eyes, but they're different coppers' eyes – his, dead fish. Hers, laser pen.

'Mr Luke Spargo?' Dead Fish asks, flashing his ID. He doesn't look at me as he speaks. 'Can I call you Luke?'

He doesn't wait for a reply. 'So, Luke, what is it you do here?'

I know they're here to check out the accounts, look at the books, I know it's nothing to do with me, nothing to do with the fire but my voice cracks anyway.

'I work at… at the counter,' I say, covering it with a cough.

He wants details. I tell him I deal with customers, general enquiries, book all jobs in, book all jobs out, order stock, keep accounts.

Laser Pen opens her mouth to say something but it's Kojak's voice that booms out. His voice is so loud it drowns out the jangle of the doorbell.

'Hey, you speak to me first. I am owner. I am the boss. Your appointment is with me, not him, nobody else. Me.'

Kojak is holding his takeaway coffee in one hand and pointing at his office door with the other.

'And before any questions happen, I need to see your warrant. Where's your warrant? I don't see one and you said you were coming back with warrant.'

'Sir, we explained all this yesterday,' Laser Pen says.

'You said you would bring. If you don't have, then goodbye.'

Kojak points backwards towards the entrance as a piece of paper gets slapped down in front of me. Kojak won't look at it, tells me to check it. It's got today's date on, the address of the garage, it's headed *WARRANT TO ENTER AND SEARCH PREMISES.*

I tell him it looks like a warrant but I've never seen one before.

'We need to ask Luke a few questions first.'

It's Dead Fish again.

'Then make it quick because he's a busy man. Like me.'

'We'll speak to Luke. You're free to go about your business as usual.'

Kojak gives me a sly wink before he walks towards his office and I hope I can remember what it is he wants me to say.

'We need to see customer details: names, addresses, contact numbers, vehicle information.'

It's Dead Fish doing the talking but it's Laser Pen I feel uneasy about.

I show them the job book. Dead Fish flips through it. 'Is everything entered by vehicle?'

I nod.

'Customer details in the job book?'

'Only telephone numbers.'

'We need to see customer details, can you show us those?'

'They're on the invoices, payment receipts, things like that.'

'Can you print a customer database, or just bring it up on screen?'

'Sorry, we don't keep digital records. Ever since the power cuts we've gone back to using paper-based documentation.'

'There haven't been any power cuts in over two years, Mr Spargo. Not since the transfer to solar power. Are you saying this company doesn't subscribe to solar power? How does your equipment function?'

'We subscribe but it's a relatively new energy source and not a proven consistent supply, so company policy is to keep written documents for a few more years.'

'If there's one thing we can be sure of, it's that the sun is going to keep on shining. It's not a novelty act. It's not going to get bored, it's not going to give up and it's not going to run out for a very long time. You should read up on it.'

I don't know why, but I thought a copper might not share the same blatant unquestioning belief. Might not belong to the same take-it-for-granted league, might not think the sun will automatically keep on doing its thing, keep on sharing the love, keep on raining down its magic.

'Is that all you've got, that one fan?' He wipes his brow and pulls at his collar.

'It is.'

'Bring us all the documentation you've got then, we'll take it away, look at it down at the station.'

A rotating card index with customer details usually sits on the desk next to the phone, but not today. Today it's gone and all the box files under the desk are gone too. That was the little something Kojak wanted help with last night. We cleared the lot, threw it all in the boot of his car.

'Apologies, but everything's with the auditors at the minute.'

'That's convenient,' he says. 'We're going to need water, lots of it. We're going to be here for some time.'

They search everywhere. Under the counter, all the cupboards, filing cabinets – there's only car mags and catalogues, vehicle reference stuff, nothing of interest. They move into the back room and I follow. They look inside the units, under the sink, in the fridge, the toilet. When they go into the workshop Malik greets them.

'Can do you guys a discount if you want. Free MOT with every service.'

They don't hang around there too long. The last place they look is in Kojak's office. He holds the door open and Dead Fish tells his partner he'll take this. Kojak's turned the air con off, they don't linger. When they're finished Dead Fish asks if we actually have any customers. I tell him we have lots of customers.

'You got evidence to support that? Because from where I'm standing it doesn't look like you have.'

I grab the job book from the front desk, show it to Dead Fish, point at today's entries. It shows car registrations, work needed, customer telephone numbers.

'It's all there, all written down,' I say.

Dead Fish's face brightens.

'Thank you very much. I think we might need to take a look at this at the station.'

He lifts the job book out of my hands and stuffs it under his arm.

'You've been most helpful, Mr Spargo.'

It feels like a set up. Feels like I've been manoeuvred into an alleyway and jumped. I look over at Kojak. He's fizzing like a dropped beer can.

Friday, 10th June 2022

It's been over a week since I last heard from Fee and I keep telling myself that it could happen. She could decide she's had enough space and text me, ring me. Everything else is hanging together. No more temperature blips, no more sign of the cops. No sightings of Mo though.

Every time I ask Malik he just says Mo's sick, and what's it to me? I nearly said, what's it to you, you mean? Malik's the one that's having to step up, put in extra hours. To be honest I'm enjoying watching him doing some proper work for once but I wish Mo would show his face because I'm sick of ringing customers up to give them the bad news. It would be easier to tell them that the sun will be coming at them like Satan with a blowtorch than say their car won't be ready as promised. Hopefully that won't happen because the sun is appeased, but I need to stay vigilant and I need to carry out further tests and that will only be possible by staying one step ahead of those with the potential to scupper that. The cops don't worry me as much as Dad, to be honest. Who knows what he's up to. Heard Mum on the phone having a sneaky chat with him again last night. I'd pissed her off because I didn't help her put the blinds up in my room like she wanted. I said I'd do it myself, told her to leave them in the room but she went on and on. Said she can't breathe when she goes in there. She could let me leave the air con on all day as well as all night but she won't. She could stay out of my room but she doesn't. Says it needs airing. Says I need to clear the shed too. She doesn't get that those stinking rotting carcasses are doing their best to save this sorry planet and her sorry arse. Like I am.

Kojak keeps fucking off and leaving me in charge. I don't mind so much now he's paying me and Malik's too busy to prat about. At least with Kojak not around and Malik stuck inside the workshop I can spend time checking for updates. The warehouse fire isn't featured any more, old news now, so unless they get new information about the guard it should fade away completely. All they've mentioned about him so far is his car. They still haven't given his name or age but like I said they could be weeding out the nutters. And there will be people ringing up making false claims. Saying they were the ones who started the fire. People will do anything for publicity, even if it means getting a life sentence.

Arsonists are the new serial killers. You start a fire and whether it takes a life or not you get life. Every government has passed that law. That's how they're viewing this, and that's how they'll view me. They won't believe my story. I'll get two life sentences. One for the fire, one for the guard. I don't care what they believe though. I can't care what others believe, can't let it stop me. I wish his family could know the truth though, but what matters is that his death meant something. It meant everything.

I'm over the road at Carlas, checking my weather app while I wait on a cheese and ham sarnie, when Fee rings. I nearly drop the phone answering it.

'Hi, how are you?'

She hasn't spoken to me since she dumped me and it's like it never happened.

'Fine.'

'Luke, I'm so sorry I've been a bit flaky. I've had so much work to do. My maths tutor is really pushing me and I had to get my assignment finished. I was already way overdue. Anyway, it's done now so I was wondering if you wanted to meet up?'

I've been waiting for this call. I kept my promise, gave her space, left her alone and it worked. She's come back and now I don't know what to say.

'I want to get back with you, Luke, I miss you. Don't you miss me?'

I don't reply for a moment. She doesn't say anything but I can feel her harden. This connection, this thing that has wrapped itself around us, it's still there.

'I've been busy too,' I say, but her soft underbelly is gone.

'Didn't take you long. What's her name?'

'Not like that. There's no one else. I've got a kind of assignment, a project of my own.'

'I'm all ears.'

'I can't talk about it,' I say. 'Not on the phone.'

'Oh, I got you, you're an undercover scientist, so why don't we go undercover?'

She taunts me with one of her squeals that sounds like a small animal, like a baby hedgehog.

'Will you have to kill me if I spill?'

I tell her I'll ring her later, when I get home. 'I've missed you too,' I say. 'Missed you a lot.'

'Not like I've missed you.'

Her voice has a small flutter. She's not playing anymore, she means it. She whispers and I try and catch what she says, have to press the phone close to my ear.

'I think I might be a tiny bit in love with you.'

It's like I've swallowed hot coals but instead of them burning me, they're filling my chest with warmth. The warmth spreads through me. It's like the feeling I get when everything's going to plan, when all the tests are going well and there's just me and the sun, working together like one unit. And now that unites me and Fee.

There's a bus stop as you step outside Carlas. Fee doesn't hear my reply because a 266 pulls up, brakes right in front of me. I say it again, shout it out loud, just as the bus comes to a halt. People at the stop stare. An old black guy, his face creased as his leather cap, takes his cap off and waves it around, lets me know he's happy for me.

I run across the road, weave in between the slowing cars.

'Love you too,' I say one more time, in case she didn't hear.

Malik's out front, smoking. He takes a last drag, flicks the tab end to the floor and crushes it under his foot. He's done it on purpose, to annoy me, but I don't care if he sets the street on fire. Fee loves me and I love her and that's all that matters. A passer-by tuts and points at a 'No Smoking' sign fastened to a nearby lamppost. As I push open the door Malik touches my arse.

'You need be careful where you stash your cash. Easy pickings, my friend.'

He's lifted two fifties from my back pocket.

'Keep them,' I say. 'I'll dock your wages. I can, now I'm in charge of finance.'

'So that was your chat with Fat Boy. I did wonder.'

I snatch the notes back, push open the door. Even the jangle doesn't sound irritating anymore. Malik follows me into the back room, sits down, rests his feet on the coffee table.

'Wouldn't get too cosy with Fat Boy.'

He's not eating anything. His break is over. He has no need to sit there. He is such a fucking ink stain. Spoils everything.

I plug my headphones into my phone and unwrap my lunch, but Malik's not done.

'Mo told me he saw you in the park.' He pumps his arms backwards and forward like I need a clue. 'Planning on running away? Getting some practice in, were we?'

I want to be left to replay the conversation. Replay what Fee said to me. Don't want that feeling to be snatched away just yet. And I don't want to be jerked back into yesterday. I drop my head and shut my eyes. Jay-Z tells me to stay happy.

'Did you give Mo some tips?' Malik lifts up one of my headphones away, talks into my left ear. 'I said, did you give my bro some tips?'

I throw my sarnie down onto the table and rip out the headphones.

'What you talking about, what tips?'

'Hey, what you think this is, charity shop? Lunchtime over ten minutes ago.'

Kojak's at the back door, panting like a dog, arms bulging with box files. He shoves the files at me. 'There's more in car.'

Malik gives me a smarmy look as I get up. His charm's so thin you could wipe it away with one finger. I put everything back where it should be. Files back under the desk, rotary index next to phone, folders back in Kojak's cabinet. All as it was. Except now they're low-fat versions. The invoices, receipts, customer cards, all thinned out. Knew by the weight of the boxes, didn't have to look.

Malik slams a set of car keys down on the counter. I pick them up and slip them onto the hook behind me. When I turn around he's still there.

'You think it's hot here. It's a fucking cauldron over in India.'

He lowers his voice and I think he's going to explain, give me a handle on what he's been talking about, but he doesn't. 'My brother's not sick, he isn't tucked up in bed at home with a cough, he's disappeared. And your new best friend's to blame.'

'It's only been a few days, he's probably sleeping on someone's floor.'

'You pretending not to have a fucking clue, or are you that dumb?'

Feels like I'm back at school, listening to the task being set, but I can't get started because I've only caught the last bit of what's been said. They wrote that on a school report once. This boy is clueless. *Clueless.* They said I didn't have what they called knowledge. I didn't know dates of when the English beat the shit out of the French, or what the capital of Malaysia was before it was something else. I know how to start a fire though. Know how to catch the sun's energy, turn it into heat. Use it to keep warm, cook food. I know how to use the sun to survive. Those fuckers don't.

I think about running after him, telling him all the things I know. What Kojak told me in his office, what Fee said. Stuff about the warehouse. The fire. Tell him the sun blazing away up there is ninety-three million miles away and that it has to travel at one hundred and eighty-six thousand miles per second just to fall on his miserable fucking face. My phone stops me. It's Mum.

  – *On split shift do spaghetti for tea make sure C eats.*

I scrape the spaghetti hoops out of the pan onto the plates. Like mine on top of the bread. Celine likes hers to the side. Celine takes her plate and disappears upstairs. I sit down on the sofa, rest my plate on my lap and wait for the news. My phone rings just as it starts.

'What you doing?' Fee asks.

'Watching TV.'

'Ask me what I'm doing.'

I ask what she's doing.

'Nothing, you've got me all to yourself. Now, ask me what I'd like to do.'

'What would you like to do?'

'You.'

My dick rises like Tower Bridge and Fee sniggers down the phone as if she can see. I think about inviting her over, think about bunging Celine a twenty, that would get rid of her for a few hours.

'Ever done phone sex?'

She doesn't wait for my reply.

'All you have to do is shut your eyes and listen.'

I press the phone tight to my ear and mute the TV. Can't mute the heavy bass coming from Celine's room but I can still hear Fee.

I listen to her in Hot Sexy Mama mode and just when I'm nearly there Celine thuds down the stairs.

'Go to go,' I say.

'I'll be at Leicester Square at half one tomorrow. Meet me,' Fee says, as Celine brings her empty plate back.

Saturday, 11th June 2022

Saturday morning always drags when I'm at work but today every time I look at the clock it says the same time. I wish we weren't meeting at Leicester Square. Not my favourite place, too many tourists.

I'm going to treat Fee. Big time. Spend some of my advance on her. Spend some of Kojak's hard-earned money on buying Fee what she wants. I clock-watch all morning. Fifteen minutes to go when she rings.

'Hey, handsome, you got plans for tonight?'

Why is she ringing to ask me what I'm doing tonight, when I'll be seeing her in less than an hour.

'Only there's a party in Hampstead and it's going to be mega. You up for it?'

Mega. It's the kind of thing Celine says. Fee's not alone, she's with a group. I recognise his voice, the guy that spoke to me, the night she rang. I ask her who she's with.

'Got to go, I'll ring you later with the info.'

'What about lunch?'

'Oh shit, I knew there was something else I was ringing you for. Sorry, can't do. See you tonight. Love you.'

Malik flicks an oil-stained rag in front of my face. It stinks. He does it again and this time I catch hold of it and pull it off him. I wrap the rag around my right hand. Dad used a tea towel. Wrapped it round his left. Southpaw. That's what he was.

'Come on then,' I say.

I put my hands up to my face like a boxer and Kojak steps out of his office.

'Go on, home,' Kojak says, locking his office door. 'Today you can both finish early.'

It's like he's doing us this big fucking favour but there's only ten minutes to go.

No one's home. I pack the usual and strap my sleeping bag to the bottom of my rucksack. I scribble a note, leave it by the kettle.

Gone Cadet training. Back Sunday.

I take the Jubilee Line at Neasden and change at Baker Street. It's packed. I'm standing near the doors next to a bunch of hyper-hyper Japanese girls. They're looking at a map of the underground, shouting out names of stops in high-pitched voices. Tot-ten-am Cot Road. Pee-ca-dee-lee. When they find Leicester Square they jump up and down and their short funky skirts frill out like mini parachutes. The tube runs overground on this stretch. It rocks and rolls along the tracks and they fall into me. They're so light they don't even dent my clothes, flutter against me like butterflies. They giggle and bunch together again, their shiny black bobs touching.

Fee rings me as we come into West Hampstead.

'Luke, listen I can — you. There's a —'

She's breaking up and I don't catch everything she says. I jump on to the platform before the tube doors close. Fee wants to tell me about the party tonight. It's a birthday party and she'll meet me at six and we can go for a drink first, then go to the party. It's her mate's seventeenth and we need to get some cans. It's in Hampstead, near the Heath, in a huge house, with a huge garden, and her mate's mum's a lawyer and her dad's a diplomat.

She doesn't take a breath, vomits the words out one after the other.

'I can't go, sorry, going away for a few days.'

It doesn't register. She carries on, tells me to meet her at Hampstead Heath and then she's gone.

Another tube train pulls into the station. It doesn't move off straight away, stays put, keeps its doors open like a basking shark. I could get on that and go do what I set off to do but instead I head for the exit. The doors slam shut behind me, and the tube whines away.

Six o'clock is over four hours away. I jump a bus, sit on the top deck next to a girl plugged into her phone. She's got a headful of braids, each one finished off with coloured beads. She nods her head along to her music and the beads tap against each other.

There's a group of guys opposite, their jackets covered in dust and paint. I'm sitting behind the main guy, the one who is doing the most talking. When he speaks he throws his hands around a lot. They're covered in nicks and grazes and he's got a nasty cut across one of his knuckles but it doesn't seem to bother him.

I must be staring because his mate across the aisle nudges him and then Knuckleman gives me a filthy look. Sometimes I do this. I don't mean to stare, I just forget. Knuckleman leans over the back of his seat and looks me up and down. He clocks the rucksack.

'What's in there?'

I turn my head to look out the window.

'Hey. I'm talking to you,' he says. 'I thought you English were polite.'

One of his mates says something and they all join in. It makes Knuckleman lean in even closer. I wish I'd stuck my headphones on so I could pretend to be listening to music like the girl next to me. Knuckleman leans so close his face almost touches mine. As he opens his mouth the smell of sour beer hits me.

'Wanna buy some good shit?' he says.

I get off the next stop with an eighth stuffed in my back pocket. Didn't want it, but I couldn't tell him that, and it could come in handy for the party. Knuckleman gives me the thumbs up from the top deck as the bus drives off.

I'm at Finchley Road, the Swiss Cottage end. Decent walk but there's no rush, still got over three hours to kill. It's an uphill climb and the sun's out and there's not a cloud to protect me. Feel the sun on my back all the way but it's way kinder. It's no way as fierce.

I head for the ponds. The mixed pond is the biggest and that should still have enough water but by the end of the summer the smaller ponds will be bone dry. I love the Heath. There are places here where you can't believe you're in London, can't even believe you're in a city. Feels like the country. Saw a hare once, and a kestrel. The kestrel flew out of a copse straight into the long grass, picked up its prey and was gone. They use their hearing to find prey. It's so good they don't need sight. In the Arctic there's a bird that can pluck things from under the snow, at night! Imagine that, thinking you're safe under a blanket of white and then *wham*. Off you go on the flight of your life. Not.

There are people swimming in the mixed pond. Boys with cut-offs doing bombs from the pont, women doing slow steady breaststroke. I lie down at the top of the small slope, rest my head on the rucksack. Everything used to be green here. The grass, the trees, even the water. I used to lie and look at the trees on the other side of the pond, look at their greenness reflected in the water. There's some yellowed patches left but it's mostly bare, gets too much traffic, like a worn carpet.

I send Fee a text, tell her to bring a sleeping bag, say I've got a better idea. Then I lie back and close my eyes. I listen to the sounds of splashing, to people jumping off the pont, having fun.

A ball slaps against my cheek, makes me sit up. It bounces away, and a kid with a fat nappy arse chases after it. The runaway ball rolls down the slope, towards the pond, shows no signs of stopping and neither does the kid.

A grubby trainer whizzes past my ear. There's a guy leaping over heads, shouting, screaming but the kid isn't taking any notice. The ball bounces into the water, drifts off towards the centre of the pond, and the kid doesn't slow down, keeps on going. Everybody's on their feet, looking to see if Dad will catch up, snatch his kid in time. One minute the kid's there in his stripy top and baggy nappy and the next he's not. The only sign he ever existed are the ripples that fan out, make the ball bob up and down.

People are running towards the pond, all expecting the same thing. Dad to dive in, rescue his son, but the stupid bastard just stands there, shouting that he can't swim. As if that's going to make it OK. As if somehow telling the whole world he can't fucking swim will stop what's happening. The swimmers in the pond head over but they're a good way off and the kid hasn't surfaced and the ripples have nearly died.

An old guy stands at the edge, gives his glasses and hat to a stranger, and jumps in fully clothed. Then two others, kids in Goth gear, do the same. Then a jogger. Then a mother. Everyone seems to be jumping in.

It's the old guy who gets him. He brings the kid up and tries to lift him in the air and nearly disappears himself. Everyone cheers. The kid's fine. Not even coughing, just got this surprised look on his face, like he doesn't know how he got so wet. The kid gets passed along a line of rescuers to his Dad and someone chucks the red ball back and I make sure it's me that catches it.

The rescue mission is huddled around Dad. I push through and hold out the ball. Dad's hugging his son so tight and kissing him so much he's making the kid squirm. The kid gives me a smile, reaches out with his chubby little hands. Dad snatches it and mutters a lame thank you.

'You need to learn to swim,' I say.

Everyone turns to look at me. I'm only saying what they're thinking. If you've got a kid you should be able to look after it. My phone rings and the kid says the word phone. He actually says 'bone' and it makes everyone smile, everyone apart from Dad.

Fee wants to know why I don't want to go to the party. Says she really wants to go and she wants me to go with her. She won't give up. I tell her she can go if she wants but I've got a better suggestion. I say I'm going to camp out on the Heath.

'I'm going to build a fire and sleep under the stars, I'd prefer some company,' I say.

She doesn't hesitate. Jumps right in. Tells me she knows some cracking places where people have made dens. Says there's a place near to where the caravans are parked, where no one really goes, we can camp there.

'And we can go look for Tilly.'

I ask who Tilly is.

'She's a squatter and she's awesome and so are you. Love you so much.'

We arrange to meet by the mixed pond at six and I set off towards East Heath. It's too wooded, too dense, not that suitable. I head west to a small patch of common. It doesn't get much footfall and there's still plenty of long grass growing wild.

I unzip a pocket of the rucksack, take out an apple and an orange. The earth and the sun. Lay them down in the middle of the long grass, a foot apart. The area's not overshadowed, so they'll get plenty of exposure. The sun should fall on them throughout the day and the grass should hide them for a good while. I offer up my thanks, and gratitude and promise always to remain a servant.

I don't linger, don't want to call attention. I turn round to take a last look, and see three girls are standing chatting just where I was. The taller one bends down and picks up the apple. I yell at her. Shout that the fruit is poisonous and she's to leave it alone. Another of them picks up the orange. I charge at them, and they scatter like mice.

I hang around, make sure the girls are gone and then I walk back towards the pond. I join a queue at one of the ice cream vans. Four vans stand beside each other. No need to compete, so much demand. A few yards away, there's another van. It's a mobile unit. The same one that was outside Willesden tube and the same medic is underneath a small canopy, handing out leaflets, signing people up, trying to steer them inside. I walk up to her with my 99. She is thrilled to see me, until she recognises me. I pick up a leaflet, fan myself with it and she turns to talk to a woman with a small child.

I find a spot under the shade of a large oak. The oaks are doing OK, roots are deeper, crowns bigger than other trees but they still struggle. Constantly shedding leaves, having to grow new ones. And the new leaves turn dry and brittle in no time. Too thirsty. Everything's too thirsty. When we run out of water that will be a fun day. There won't be anyone handing out leaflets or wanting to help. It won't be very civilised, won't be very English. It'll be fucking carnage.

I see Fee before she sees me. She's carrying a sleeping bag and four cans of beer. She's wearing a long hippy looking dress, and she's put glittery stuff around her eyes. It makes her look older, and I'm not sure if I like it.

I take her sleeping bag and she slips her arm through mine and kisses me on the cheek. I turn my face towards her and kiss her on the lips. She's had a spliff, can smell the sweetness.

'You've been smoking.'

'I know. Do you want a sneaky roll-up?'

'No thanks,' I say. 'And you shouldn't smoke outside. It's still banned.'

'You want to build a fire, how you going to get away with it?'

'Trust me, I'm good at hiding fires. I don't smoke anyway and I don't drink.'

She swings her cans at me. 'So, what *do* you do? I mean you must do something, you must have some bad habits. Apart from me.'

I tell her she's pissed and she runs off, arms stretched wide, like a plane. I chase after her, throw her sleeping bag at the back of her legs. It catches her behind her knees and she falls. I fall on top of her, pin her outstretched arms to the ground. Her dress is low cut at the back. Can see her shoulder blades, her spine.

'What you doing?'

'Examining your back, it's a bit red,' I say. 'You need to be careful.'

'Dear Lord, I am but a poor sinner. I smoke, I drink, I sunbathe. Strike me down, oh Lord, strike me down.'

I let go of her and she rolls onto her back and pulls her dress up.

'I know what kind of sinner you are,' she says.

Her dress is hitched right up to her knickers. I tell her we're in a park. She doesn't care. She puts a hand to her crotch and I grab hold of her, drag her to her feet.

'How much have you smoked?'

She squirms away from me. 'Fuck you, Mr Goody Goody. Mr Too Goody, Fucking Two Shoes. You want to try it, I'd recommend it, washes everything away. All the crap, all the crud, all the sins. See, there they go. Glug, glug, glug.'

Her face is criss-crossed from the prickly grass, and a few blades are stuck to her cheek. I grab her wrist, pull her towards me. She doesn't resist, falls into me, soft as feathers. We walk through the Heath looking for the place Fee is sure exists.

'This way, yeah, it's this way. I remember now.'

She runs past a row of uprooted trees. The way they lie, roots ripped from the ground, branches twisting into the air, you can see it was some fight. Fee shouts 'Catch!' and chucks her four-pack at me but I'm too busy looking at the battered trees and I miss. We're at the top of a slope and the cans fall to the ground and roll away. Roll all the way to the bottom.

'Go fetch, butterfingers,' Fee says.

I walk off down the slope, take my time. The ground is worn, dry. You can lose your footing easy on this kind of surface. When I get to the bottom I pick up the cans and walk back.

Fee's not there. I look around, call her name but she doesn't reply. I jump up onto an upturned tree to get a better look but there's no sign of her. Opposite is a wooded bit and I try and see if I can spot her in amongst the bushes and the trees. I think I catch sight of her dress but it's a guy in a long shirt.

She could have gone for a piss or she could be playing a stupid game. Maybe that's it, maybe she's hiding, wants me to find her. I shout her name again, tell her to stop messing about, tell her to show herself but she's gone. Disappeared, just like the kid at the pond.

I don't know whether to stay put or go looking. If I move she might come back and then she won't know where I am.

A woman has been hanging around at the edge of the wood while I've been considering this. From the way she's dressed, and the way she looks, I'm guessing she's an open-air dweller. It's a better title than homeless but it means the same thing.

'I haven't got any money,' I say, jumping down from the upturned tree.

'Don't want your money.'

She's got a strange accent, to go with her strange look. She goes to say something more but I head off into the wood.

The deeper I go the thicker the trees get and the less light there is. The woman's been following me all the while. I turn around, tell her to get lost and she stands still and points.

'There she be,' she says. 'Over there, look.'

I look to my left and see her. Fee's sitting in a tree, on one of the low hanging branches, waving. The woman grins, and I see her yellow teeth are the same colour as her frizzy hair.

Fee drops down from the tree and runs towards me, carries on straight past and flings her arms around the woman.

'Thank you, Tilly.'

'Thars alright, but you mighta told me though.' The woman shoots me a look. 'She said you were 'ansome an' fair but she forgot to say you weren't all there.'

I look at Fee, wait for an explanation, but she just grins at me too.

'OK, lover, I'll be orff now, getting a bit late for me, usually eat well afore now. Catch yous later.'

We're standing in a small clearing and there's a tepee, made from lengths of silver birch. The ground in front of it is blackened from a past fire.

Fee and the woman kiss each other on the cheek and then the woman walks off. Her thin frizzy hair bounces with each step.

'Bye, Tilly. Say hello to Baxter from me,' Fee shouts.

'Who's that?'

'Baxter's her dog.'

'I didn't mean the dog, I meant the mad woman.'

'FYI Tilly's my friend. I sent her to find you and she did. She brought you here and all you can do is be rude.'

She holds out her hand for her bag. I give it to her.

'I should go to the party.'

'Fine,' I say, 'let's go.'

'I said *I* should. I didn't say you.'

'I was worried, thought you'd got lost. Sorry, I didn't mean to upset you.'

I unroll my sleeping bag in front of the tepee and Fee sits down on it and rips opens a can of lager. The froth shoots out and spills over her hand. Any other time she'd find that funny and we'd both laugh.

She roots through her bag again. 'Did the dope fall out?'

'Must have,' I say.

'Shit. May as well stay here and drink beer then.'

I think about giving her the eighth in my back pocket. I know it would please her, get me back in her good books but I want to save it for Celine. She knows more than she's letting on about Dad.

'You're not supposed to light fires in public places, you do know that. What if a firespotter catches us?'

'They've relaxed the rules now the temperatures have fallen, which is just as well because how else we going to eat this lot.'

I show her the food I brought from home, the sausages, onions, rolls. The tin plates and frying pan. She's well impressed and helps to collect enough kindling to get a fire going. I'll need to collect some decent wood, to keep the fire burning into the night. Wish I could tell her the real reason. That I need the firelight to keep me company while I sleep. That it's my nightlight.

The sausages don't take long to cook, they're cheap and run with fat, which makes browning the onions a cinch and they taste great. We have two sausage sandwiches each.

'You're such a mashup of boy scout and mad scientist,' Fee says. 'Very nearly perfect but you forgot to bring sauce.'

'Do you think they'll come back? The people that built the tepee?' I say, swallowing the last mouthful.

'Nope, it's been here ages, they've left it for waifs and strays like us to use. But I am surprised the firespotters haven't destroyed it.'

'Do they really exist? There's plenty of talk about them but I've never seen one.'

'Aren't they supposed to be covert. Work in plain sight, like a private detective.'

I pick up her beer from the ground, flick some lager at the fire. The flames spit and Fee screams, nearly drops her food.

'Don't. I'm a bit scared of fires to be honest,' she says. 'Never really had bonfires as a kid. I'm glad they banned them, to be honest.'

'Bonfires are amazing. Have you seen the videos, the old footage from the millennium? Those shots up and down the country, everyone standing around the blazing fires.'

She shakes her head and I say I'll show her sometime.

When I found the old clips, I watched them over and over. Wished I could have been there, witnessed it at first hand. Pockets of light bursting to life, one after the other, like a giant runway all the way up the spine of England. That's how they were described: *the Peaks, the Moors, the Downs, all lit up by a shower of shooting stars, fallen to earth.*

Was such a big event. People crying, hugging each other. You could see there was a buzz, an energy that spread like the fires. Could hear it in the voices, see it in the faces. They were using fire to connect, to unite with each other, with the earth, the sky, the universe. The power of ritual.

I tell Fee I need to gather more wood whilst it's still light. There's about another hour left and I want to get it built up by the time the dark falls. I collect some branches, thicker than before but thin enough to snap with my foot. When I've built enough to keep the fire going I sit beside her.

She looks at me and I see the reflection of the flames in her pupils and as she moves towards me the firelight dances across her face. It casts long spidery shadows down her cheeks and I know this is all I want. This is all I need.

We kiss and I move my hand up her leg, slip my fingers inside her knickers. Can hear the sound of rustlings – foxes, rabbits? Whatever, we're the same as them. Night-mating like animals. Fee cries out and the fire crackles and spits as if it's jealous.

Afterwards we lie naked, smelling of sex and smoke.

'Maybe we should think about using something next time,' I say.

'It's sorted, I have a regular injection.'

'You know what I mean.'

'You're a virgin and I always get checked when I get my jab. It's fine, don't worry I'm not going to give you anything nasty.'

I ask her about her first time. She tells me it was at a festival and the guy wasn't too happy about it. She was only fourteen.

'Maybe that's why he wasn't too happy,' I say.

'I didn't tell him I was that young, I said I was sixteen. Didn't want to be the last virgin in the class. He said I was using him, when he realised it was my first time. You guys can fake being a virgin but our womanly bodies give us away. Send out a red warning signal. We get all the good biology.'

'Were you using him?'

'Doesn't everybody at some time use someone?'

I say I'm not using her.

'You sure about that? You can be honest, I won't mind. It's just sex.'

Sounds like something Malik would say. I have the crazy thought that they might know each other. Like really know each other.

'Speak to me. I don't like it when you go quiet.'

I tell Fee about what happened at the pond earlier, with the ball. She got that it wasn't about the kid, that it wasn't about him falling in and getting rescued, it was about the Dad. About how useless the Dad was.

'He was such a fucking idiot.'

'You talking about your Dad, or the kid's Dad?'

She's so good at joining the dots. So good at making sense of stuff.

'I know you mentioned you don't really get on with him but you haven't said much else.'

'My Dad was a bully. He fucked with my head. Ended up having to see a school shrink.'

'Shit, Luke.'

'Waste of fucking time that was. First time we met him he kept me waiting outside his office, so I drew on the back of the registration form to pass the time. He asked what the doodles meant and when I said they didn't mean anything he said everything has meaning, even a doodle.'

'What did you draw?'

'An apple. With an Egyptian eye inside it. He folded the form up and stuck it in his back pocket.'

'Bet he wiped his arse with it.'

It feels good, telling her this, being able to laugh about it, instead of fucking crying. It feels safe, feels right and it feels like I could tell her more.

Sunday, 12th June 2022

Fee's standing over me looking none too happy. I rub the sleep from my eyes, try and see what's upset her.

'You some kind of terrorist?' she asks.

I prop myself up on my elbows.

'I was looking for the torch last night, needed to pee, and I found all this bombmaking shit.'

She picks my rucksack up, tips it upside down. The front flap falls open like a busted jaw and everything crashes out. Mirrors, sugar, newspapers, hammer.

'You didn't need to go snooping, the torch was in the side pocket. I told you that,' I say.

A bag of sugar has burst open. I get up and aim a kick at it. Then another and another.

Feel sick. Feel stupid and sick. She won't look at me. Fiddles with her hair, pulls it into a tight ponytail.

'Well, I'm waiting,' she says.

'I'm testing the sun's power. I test the sun rays, start fires, work out how strong it is. Compare the results over time.'

'I can tell you how strong it is. I can tell you what the temperature is right now if you want me to.'

I mimic her, say I've got the same app.

'I don't mean to make fun of you. If it means that much to you, tell me about it. I want to know.'

I show her my notebook. Show her the stats, the ignition times, the drawings. Tell her I've got records going back years.

'Wow, you have done your research,' she says.

'I've got more notebooks at home,' I say, 'and it's all on my PC, got a customised database.'

'I'd like to see it sometime,' she says.

We stand opposite each other, the roadkill of sugar between us. There's a troop of ants on it already. It's military, the way they fetch and carry the crystals. Lines and lines of them, all doing the same thing, each one passing the load to the next. I squat down and tell her to be careful, not to tread on them.

'They must think their birthday and Christmas have come all at once,' she says, kneeling beside me.

I turn and look at her. Her eyes are soft. It's enough.

We find a café on Hampstead High Street. It's trendy, expensive, but they do fry-ups. We order two cooked breakfasts, one with mushrooms, one without. The waitress reads our order back to us and she makes it sounds like it's such a fucking surprise. Must be an Aussie. She's all in black, except for a little white pinny. Her uniform goes with her short black hair and super white teeth. As she's about to go, I ask for extra tomatoes.

'No worries,' she beams.

They're like that, Aussies. Bright. Sunny. I smile back. Fee smiles at her too. It's not a friendly smile though.

We haven't said much since the sugar incident and it feels like she's going to say something about it again, ask me more things.

'How do you know Tilly?' I ask.

'Don't you mean Mad Bitch?'

Fee pushes her hair back from her face. She's much prettier than the waitress. Everything about her is better than the waitress.

'She was our neighbour, lived two doors down. She used to be an actor. That voice she put on last night, it's not her real one, talks in accents all the time. She used to slip into a Scottish accent if she didn't like someone.'

'Why?'

'When you say couldn't in a Glaswegian accent it sounds like cunt. Go on, give it a go.'

I tell her I'm not very good at accents but she wants me to try.

'You cun't pass me the sauce, could ya. Sorry, no I cun't and even if I wanted to, I cun't cos I'm stuck to this wee cunt of a chair.'

Then Fee has a go and she's good but she's loud and all the while she's doing it the Aussie waitress is flicking me looks. She's wiping down a table at the back of the café and keeps eyeing me from under her thick fringe. She's late twenties, early thirties, and I can't help wondering what it would be like with someone older.

'I'm over here,' Fee waves.

I tell her that she's really good at accents. 'Ever thought about being an actor?'

'Maybe *you* should. Because you're doing a good impression of not wanting to jump that waitress.'

Fee and the waitress exchange a look.

'Whatever she can do, I can do ten times better,' Fee says.

An image of her and the waitress, naked, fighting over me, lands in my head. I pick up the jug of water on the table and pour us both a drink.

Our breakfasts arrive and it's a different waitress that brings them. I dip my toast into the sloppy shiny egg, watch the yolk seep out. I look at it, all the food on my plate. The beans, the mushrooms, the tomatoes, the sausage, the bacon, the eggs.

Everything tastes great when you've got a hunger on you, but nothing beats a fry-up. Won't matter how hot it gets, the fry-up won't disappear from the menu. The only sounds we make come from eating and we don't stop until we've cleaned our plates. The other waitress takes them away and asks if we want anything else. Fee says she'd like an iced tea, then looks at me as if I should have one too. I say, same here, even though I don't want one.

There's a salt pot on the table. Fee picks it up and pours enough out to make a small pyramid, which she flattens once she's made it and then makes more shapes with the salt. She makes a square, a triangle and a circle. Then she makes a long thin white line. She dips her head and pretends to snort it.

I take a check to see if anyone's seen her. The café is packed and everyone's busy with each other, or their food, but Aussie waitress is looking over at us. I smile but she doesn't smile back. It's hot and humid in the café. There's plenty of overhead fans but the air con isn't on. Soon as temps drop and solar alerts disappear the first thing people do is stop using their air con. Should be a health and safety requirement in public places, especially cafés and restaurants. Every time the kitchen door opens there's a blast of heat. I feel for the poor bastards having to work in there.

Fee blows at the white line and salt skits across the Formica. I blow it back at her and she returns the favour. We play blow salt until we go dizzy.

'When I saw all that sugar, I thought you were planning on baking me a cake,' Fee says. 'Little did I know, you were a practising fire starter.'

There's a TV on the far wall. Chalk menu boards either side of it. A programme on community firespotters is playing. Shows how they recruit volunteers and who is eligible to apply. You have to be sixteen and over with no criminal history. That's about it. They stress it's nothing like the role of the emergency services. There's no tackling fires, no attendances at fires. It's about spotting and reporting and being watchful for any situation that could potentially lead to a fire. This café could be a potential situation. All you need is heat, air and a fuel source.

It's just another con, another tactic, a side-blinding strategy to make it look like they're doing something, make it look like they're taking control of the situation. The best form of deflection is to create a false enemy, lure everyone away from the real one.

'No. More. Secrets.'

Fee snaps her fingers in front of my face, in time to the words.

'No. More. Secrets. No. More. Secrets.'

Aussie waitress brings the iced teas over.

'I'm sorry it's taken so long, clean forgot about them.'

I like that she owns up, admits to ballsing up. There's no shame attached. It's just her being honest. She flashes me another of her bright Aussie smiles. I flash her one back and Fee kicks my leg, catches me right on the shin. It's annoying, the way she does this when she's not pleased with something I do or say.

'Believer or Unbeliever?' I say.

'You fancy her, don't you?'

'Answer the question.'

'Stop looking at her.'

'I'm looking at the TV,' I say.

'Liar.'

She kicks me again. This time I reach down, grab hold of her foot and give it a good yank. She slips down her chair and I yank it again and she kicks me right in the crotch. I swear at her and she swears back. Bitch. Bastard. Wanker. Cunt.

Everything freezes, all the talking and eating noises stop and Aussie waitress marches over with the bill. We are to pay up and leave. The bill is five pence short of fifteen pounds. I claw a twenty-pound note out of my trouser pocket, throw it on top of the bill. The waitress holds the door open for us. Her breezy smile gone.

Another fucking Ungrateful I wish I hadn't saved.

We walk away. I'm limping and Fee is sulking. She tells me she hates it when I'm in a mood and I tell her I hate it when she behaves like a kid and kicks me in the balls. She wants to call round and see if the party's still going. Fortune's parties have been known to go on all weekend, she says.

'Her parents go away a lot so she has lots and lots of parties. Shit, I wish I hadn't lost that dope. We can't go empty-handed. Not to a party.'

I reach into my back pocket, show her the eighth.

'Oh, you star! You absolute fucking star!'

I tell her about the bus, about Knuckleman.

'Good work,' she says, going to take it.

'It'll be safer with me,' I say and shove it back into my pocket.

'You will absolutely love Fortune, and she'll absolutely love you. She's a princess, really she is. She's a Nigerian princess.'

'Cool name,' I say.

I've never met a princess before, Nigerian or otherwise. I try and get a handle on the people I might meet, what they might talk about, and Fee carries on. It's like she's been given a set of new batteries. I tune back in, pick up her conversation.

'Her Dad likes cars, the old fashioned type, the classic ones, and they've got all this art. Like, original, famous shit. Damien Hirst pictures and I think they might have a Banksy. And they've got this amazing African art too. All these carvings and, well, they're just such interesting people, can't wait for them to meet you.'

'Are you taking stuff?' I ask. 'Hard drugs style stuff.'

'What?'

'Sometimes you seem so wired, so high.'

She stops dead in the street.

'It's you,' she says. 'You make me like this. You're my drug.'

She does it again, takes a pin to all my worries, pops them like they're soap bubbles.

Fortune's road is one of those wide, tree-lined ones. The kind with serious cars parked on serious drives. One house is set so far back from the road you could fit another between it and the pavement. Only seen houses like that in magazines. Didn't think they actually existed. It's a crescent and as we walk along the curve a police car comes into view.

'That's Fortune's house,' Fee says, pointing at a gated house. The gate is open and as if by magic, the front door of the house opens as we look at it and someone steps out. It's a cop. We've summoned up a cop. As he walks towards the car he drops his head and speaks into his radio. Fee wants to find out what's going on. Wants to go and ask the copper. Even though he's got a gun pinned to his hip, she wants to go and talk to him. I tell her it's none of our business, but I can see how excited she is. She's turned into a rubbernecker, can't help but be drawn in.

I hide behind one of the trees as she walks towards the copper. They stand by the car chatting. As the copper gets into the car he turns and looks in my direction. I jerk my head back behind the tree. Can't risk being seen, can't risk being questioned. They're nosy bastards, coppers, proper nosy bastards. He'll want my name, address, number. He'll want to check out my bag and I risk him searching my bag. He'll know what sugar and mirrors can do. All it would take is a quick search. Suspicious fires. Possible arson attack. The warehouse fire would be the first thing it would find.

I reach home within the hour. Fee's been ringing, texting, all the way. Wants to know where I am, what happened, why I left. She tells me the house got trashed because news about the party got out and a heap of gatecrashers turned up and now Fortune's in such deep shit. Suddenly Fortune's name doesn't sound so cool anymore. I text her back to say I had the dope in my back pocket, that's why I left. I say her I'll ring later then switch my phone off. I need to get rid of the cuttings and the mirrors ASAP, and the notebooks. I need to destroy all evidence. This was a warning. My final warning.

Even before I open the wardrobe, I know something's not right. The door needs a good push to shut it properly. I always do that. I always make sure it's closed. I never leave it open. Not even a tiny bit and I never leave it like this. I never leave it ajar. I swing the door open and push the clothes hanging on the rail out of the way. The box file is where it usually is, at the bottom of the wardrobe, pushed right to the back, hidden underneath a pile of old jumpers. But it's lying face up. I always put lay it face down. Never face up. I take it out, check the cuttings.

I left the latest article, the one with the map, on the top because it's the newest, and it holds the other cuttings nicely in place, because it's a double page spread. That's still there, still at the front, where it should be, but the others aren't where they should be. Everything was in date order, newest to oldest, but now they're all jumbled up.

Monday, 13th June 2022

There was a news bulletin on the BBC this morning. *Tempers rise in line with temperatures.* A university research team has spent two years and thousands of pounds to come to this conclusion, when all they had to do was take a ride on public transport. Course people's tempers rise when the heat goes up. It's called the pressure cooker theory.

There was a fight on the bus this morning. Someone sat too close to someone else and it ended up in a punch up. I got off and walked the rest of the way to work. It can be worse on the tube, the Central Line's the worst. Some clever bastard renamed it Fight Central. Social media is where they should be looking. Tempers are always rising there, no matter what the temperature is. Believers and Unbelievers constantly techno jousting, throwing their stupid theories at each other. But that's what they want, those in charge. They want the constant chattering, the forever noise. They're never happier than when we're scrapping, and they make sure that's what we do.

That's all Malik wants to do lately. Been in a foul mood all morning. Kept skulking around reception like he wanted to talk to me, hung around like a wasp at a fucking picnic but when I asked him what he wanted, he bit my head off.

'My brother, the one that works here, he's still missing, in case you hadn't noticed.'

Malik jabs at finger towards Kojak's office.

'He's to blame for that. Him and his dodgy dealings bringing the police sniffing around. Making promises he's never going to keep.'

'What promises?'

'Don't play the innocent, it doesn't suit you. You and Kojak all cosy cosy and you're pretending not to know? You know full well what he's promised. A passport, a fucking passport, that's what. Mo's an illegal and Kojak's got him by the balls. You really think Kojak makes money from this two-bit garage? This is a front, he's got his finger in a much bigger pie. Him and Irish got a nice little passport scam set up. The cars we service for the taxi business, they used to ship the money and the passports backwards and forwards. Kojak must be putting the money through the garage accounts, and the police must have sussed it. He's set you up too, that promotion, it's to cover his arse. Nice little earner though, eh? All those overheated countries, why wouldn't you try and leave. Mo won't survive if they send him back to India.'

As he walks away the phone rings. It's Irish. He doesn't want to speak to Kojak which is just as well as he's not here, he just wants me to pass on a message.

I ring Kojak and tell him what Irish said. He asks me to repeat it.

'Is that all he said?'

I say yes.

I can hear the fear in his voice. Never thought anything would scare Kojak. But scared he is.

'Three o'clock deadline, or Curtis. Your choice,' I say again.

'OK, this is what you need to do.'

I listen to his instructions and write down the six numbers he gives me on the back of my hand.

It's awkward, because of its size, but it's not that heavy. I lift it away from the wall and rest it against Kojak's desk. The map's been there for some time and it's left a mark on the coffee coloured paintwork, which in itself acts as a frame to the small square safe cut into the wall.

Was expecting something bigger. Something with a dial and a spinning wheel of a lock. Kojak's safe is the size of a laptop with a ten-digit keypad and a big solid handle but I've never seen a real life safe before, so I'm not too disappointed. It's still making the back of my neck prickle.

I punch in the six numbers 8-3-3-7-5-1 then press the hash key and twist the handle clockwise. The door is solid and opens slowly. Inside are the passports that Kojak wants me to give to Irish but that's not all that's in there. The safe is stuffed full of money. Wads of notes are rammed inside. Squashed up against each other. They're fifty pound notes. Must be five grand a bundle. I tease one out, hold it up to the light like I'm an expert in fakery, a real live gangster.

I ring Irish. He doesn't say anything when he answers the call but I can hear the impatience in his breathing.

'All sorted, everything's ready for pick up,' I say.

He makes a smug little sound and then he ends the call.

I put the passports into a jiffy bag, sellotape it shut. It takes less than half an hour for someone to turn up. I'm not sure whether I should have suggested a code word for collection but the guy who comes to pick them up comes straight out with it. He's dressed head to foot in designer sportswear, got on a pair of white baggy leggings and a gold hoodie. He keeps his hood up and doesn't take his Raybans off.

'Got the goods?' he asks.

I hand him the jiffy bag and he hands it right back to me.

'I ain't got X-ray eyes, man.'

I've stuck the sellotape down too well and I can tell he's enjoying the fact I have to cut it open with scissors. I show him the contents and he takes the opened jiffy, unzips his hoodie, shoves it inside and zips it up again.

'I take it Curtis won't be coming,' I say.

I can feel him staring through his Raybans. 'Not today, he's busy elsewhere.'

I tell Malik he needs to padlock the workshop and leave by the back gate, because I've locked the main building up.

'Alright for some,' he says. 'What I said earlier, about you needing to be careful. If Kojak goes down, he'll take you with him.'

I ring Kojak on the way home. He says I've done good and then he gives me a little warning, tells me he hopes he can trust me to keep this between us. I tell him I don't know what he's talking about. He laughs, says he'll see me in the morning and then adds, he knows exactly how much money was in the safe.

I go home via Sainsbury's and B&Q and get everything I need.

Mum's taking Celine shopping for yet another birthday present, so they won't be back until half six. Gives me plenty of time to set up.

Celine's first to see me, catch her face in the kitchen window. But it's Mum who's first out.

'What are you doing?'

I'm in the back garden wearing an apron, holding a set of tongs in one hand, standing in front of an unlit barbeque, so it's a fair question. Celine joins us, stands next to Mum. They're like clones of each other. Both dressed exactly the same. White top, denim shorts, straw boater.

'Have they lifted the ban?'

I make out I didn't catch what Celine said, so Mum says it, and I'm sure I hear her stutter. Mum looks at the table. I bought sausages, burgers, chicken wings, bread buns and paper plates, sauces and serviettes. Everything's there.

'It's only a pretend barbie. I'll cook it all on the grill inside and bring it out. Thought it would be good to do something as a family,' I say.

Mum pats the serviettes, still in their wrapping, then examines the chilli sauce.

'You forgot the chairs,' Celine announces and runs back inside.

Mum puts the sauce back down on the table, picks up the chicken wings. She's like a detective looking for clues.

'Where were you last night?'

She used the same tone with Dad. She'd try and hide it, but the suspicion cut through every word like a wire.

'Nice being outside, isn't it, now it's cooler,' I say. 'We might get to spend time outside in the sun and not have to keep dodging out of its way.'

Celine's head pops over Mum's shoulder. She stretches one arm out to the side to show she's holding a bottle of brown sauce, turning Mum into a two headed, three-armed monster.

'Thought you were getting chairs,' I say.

She slaps her forehead with the heel of her palm like she's oh-so-dumb and disappears off again. I joke with Mum that she's like a bloody yo-yo, always in and out. Mum picks up the serviettes and rips them open. There's a slight breeze and it lifts the wrapper off the table into the air, plays with it for a while and then drops it like a bored kid.

'Chicken or beef burger?' I say.

Mum weights the serviettes down with knives and forks, asks me where I was last night. I tell her I was at a training session with Cadets.

'I left you a note,' I say.

'I didn't think you went to Cadets anymore. You never talk about them.'

'It was a one-off session. We went on a night hike through London.'

'Don't lie to me, Luke.'

'I'm not, why would I?'

'Because you sleep with a night light on and you won't have any curtains up at your window because you don't like dark, that's why I don't believe you.'

'I made myself go because I need to grow up, get over it. Isn't that what he used to say? Well, I'm trying to do that. You should be thanking me, encouraging me. And we went together. It's being alone in the dark, that's what I don't like. I'm OK if there's someone else around.'

Mum's mouth tightens.

'Whatever the reason is, Luke, I don't want you staying out all night. I know you're an adult, you're over eighteen, but you're not to do it again, not while you're living in this house.'

It's him speaking, not her. That's the kind of cliched thing he'd say. She stares at the ground as if she's lost something, the way she does when she drops an earring on the carpet. Celine appears with two dining chairs. She drags them behind her and the metal legs scrape across the patio.

'He was with his girlfriend.'

Mum's eyes ping-pong between me and Celine.

'Her name's Fee.'

Celine shuffles the chairs under the table and slaps her hands together like everything's fine. The scraping sound has moved inside my head. It should be me dropping in the surprise, not her, not Celine. The cuttings, the warehouse fire, I can deal with her knowing about that, I can deal with her snooping around in my room, looking for something to get over on me. I can sort that. But announcing Fee's name, coming out with it like that, like she knows her, like she's met her. And now that Mum knows, Dad will, and she'll be gone, the one thing that matters because he destroys everything that matters, that really matters.

'And he's put a lock on his door!' Celine shouts.

Snoop Dog Sista can't stop. She's just going to keep on. I grab hold of her, drag her down the garden, drag her all the way to the bottom. I've got her in a headlock, my arm wrapped tight around her head.

'You dare tell Mum what you found, you dare tell her about the cuttings and I'll tell her about your dirty little secret.'

Celine begs me to let her go. She's teary and snotty just like Mo. I tighten my grip.

'Understand?' I say.

Mum's reached us, she's throwing her fists into my back, shouting at me to let go. I'm about to but Celine sinks her teeth into my wrists and I punch her. I don't punch her hard, it's more a reaction to being bitten than anything, but it makes her nose bleed. Mum pulls me away and hugs Celine. Celine buries her head in Mum's chest and it looks like Mum been shot. A huge red stain spreads out across her white top.

'Get out! Get out of my house and don't come back!' Mum shouts.

I back away, grab a handful of serviettes from the table to wipe the blood from my arm, and run.

My clothes are stuck to me by the time I get to the park. I take my usual route, up the hill towards the bowling green, once around the green, and back down the hill. When I near the bridge I run along the train tracks and sit underneath the arch. I lean back against the brick wall and ring Fee. I ask if I can see her, meet her, now. Come over she says, no hesitation.

'Mum's not here at the minute so we'll have the house to ourselves.'

She gives me her address, spells out the road name and the postcode. I don't remind her I already know where she lives. I already followed her home. I tell her I'll see her soon.

'Something wrong, you had a fall-out?'

'Kind of.'

'Love you,' she sings.

I tell her I love her back.

The sun is bronzing the tracks and the houses that run alongside it. I get up and walk towards it. Towards the one thing that will always have my respect. My loyalty lies with you, will always lie with you, I say. I will never betray you because you have never betrayed me. You have not deserted us, you have never left us. But I know you can and I know if you did, that punishment would be final.

It's like when I watched from behind the car, only this time it's me standing on the doorstep, I'm stepping into the house. I follow Fee down the hall. It's dark and narrow and I have to watch my step to avoid the stuff lined up against the skirting boards. Shoes, boots, bags full of clothes, empty boxes, magazines.

Fee flicks the light on in the kitchen. It's messy and colourful and nothing matches. Books piled everywhere, notepads, pens, pencils, opened bills, letters. If Mum was here she'd be wearing her worried face. Clutter doesn't sit well with her.

Fee fills a water jug at the sink. The tap makes a whining sound, then shudders shut. She puts it in the fridge and takes out a chilled one.

'I'm glad they lifted the water ban. Hate buying bottled water. Tap water's fine. And I hate not being able to shower every day. I sweat far too much.'

She pours out two glasses of water, hands me one. 'Come on, what's up. Something's bugging you.'

'Can we go to bed?'

'Sure. Sex is always a good antidote to feeling shit.'

Fee picks up the drinks and I follow her upstairs. The house is like a version of her. Busy, messy. Everything's a mismatch but it works. It all works. We have sex and she's right. It works. It makes me feel much better.

'You're hooked on it now, aren't you?'

'I'm hooked on you,' I say.

'Apparently the heat is making people have more sex. Heard it on the news, everyone's at it. It's lighting fires inside as well as outside. Our neighbour's shed exploded the other day. They were storing paint in there.'

'Dumb thing to do,' I say.

'It's a crime now, being fire safety negligent. Did you know?'

I say I didn't and tell her I'm tired, I need to sleep. She goes for a shower and I close my eyes. Listen to the sound of the shower, imagine it's raining outside, imagine the splish-splash of rain on the windowsill. The shower fades away and the rain gets heavier. Big fat drops are dancing around my head, waking up all the thoughts I'd put to sleep. I try and focus, try and remind myself of what I've achieved. Out of everyone, I'm the one that was chosen and I'm the one that's going to fix everything. And then the rain stops and the sun comes out. Stays out all day, all night, never ever sets and I'm happy because it means I'll never have to worry, I'll never have the fear of it going out, because it will always be there. But the heat stays too, that never goes away and it builds hotter and hotter, and the air gets thicker and thicker, until there's this yellow fog. Everyone but me is wearing gas masks. They have to, it's the only way they can breathe, the only way they can see. A man, a patrol officer, tries to give me a mask but I tell him I don't need one. He's insistent, keeps pushing it at me, and I see who it is. It's him. It's Dad. He points at me says it's my fault, that me being afraid of the dark has caused this. Me wanting to keep a light on has brought this on. Everyone stops to listen to him and then they point at me. I hear them shouting *Burn him! Burn him!* as a huge drop of rain falls from the sky. It grows bigger and bigger, heavier and heavier as it comes closer.

'You OK?'

I'm bolt upright in bed and Fee's beside me, stroking my arm.

'I used to have nightmares,' she says, as if it's a choice. 'You can tell me about it if you want. You know what they say, a trouble shared is a trouble halved.'

'It's a problem shared, not a trouble,' I say.

'Trouble, problem, same thing in my book. Me, I'm the good fairy of troubles and problems, all you have to do is tell me what's up and I will help make it go away.'

'Do you know how annoying that is, making out you can wave a magic wand and everything will be fine?'

'Fuck you. I'm going to sleep.'

Fee moves as far away as she can, lies right on the edge of the bed. I roll away from her, punch the pillow into a ball under my head. There's a poster of Che Guevara on her wall. All people see is the beret, the hair, the looks. They don't see the pain. The fucking hurt staring right at you. It's there in his eyes, all you have to do is look.

Tuesday, 14th June 2022

Fee's already put a breakfast bowl out for me. She asks if I want cereal, then tells me that's all there is. I fill my bowl with Rice Krispies and pour on the milk. Fee finds it funny when I put my ear to the bowl.

'Wasn't allowed these as a kid. Dad banned them because the snap crackle and pop got on his nerves. He called them a time-wasting novelty.'

'Why?'

'We took too long to eat them because we spent too long listening.'

'That was mean of him.'

'He did things like that all the time.' I take a spoonful of cereal. 'He's sending Celine money for her birthday.'

'And.'

'It's fucking with my head.' The krispies don't stay crisp too long but I don't care that they're soggy. 'It's been great not having him around all this time and now suddenly he wants to be there. I know what he's up to, he's going to try and wheedle himself in. And Mum and Celine, they'll fall for it and he'll step right back into his old ways.'

'How long's it's been since you saw him?'

'Eight years. Eight years without once having to look at that face, hear that voice.'

'That's enough time to reflect, have regrets. He might be sorry for what he did, might want to apologise.'

'He made my life hell, he ruined my fucking childhood. How can an apology undo that?'

'You could forgive him. You shouldn't hold on to bad shit. Forgiveness isn't about letting someone off with what they've done, it's about saying I'm done with it. It's over.'

I have to ball my hands into two tight fists to stop myself from shoving them into her mouth and stop her preaching her psychobabble.

As if a blackout blind has been dropped, all the light disappears from the room and we get plunged into darkness. Fee reaches up to put the light on and I see him peering into my room, his hand on the light switch, that stupid drunken smile on his face. Now you see me, now you don't, he says as he flicks the switch on and off.

If he'd stopped at that, if all I had to do was lie in the dark on piss-soaked sheets, that would have been OK. I could have handled that. Could have handled the warnings, the threats. I would have laid there and never been tempted to climb up on the chair and put the light back on. But he couldn't stop there. Why would he? When all it would take to blow my whole fucking world apart was one throwaway sentence. The sun could go out just as easy, he'd say, as he flicked off the switch for the last time.

Fee grabs a hairbrush from the fruit bowl that is filled with anything but fruit.

'I have a question regarding your tattoo, sir. Was it your love of the sun and all things hot that made you a fan of the unholy gods, or was it the other way around?'

She's using the brush as a microphone and she's speaking in a pushy American voice.

'Could you please tell me the story behind it.'

I rip the brush from her hands and throw it down on the table. It catches the edge of the bowl and cracks it.

'That's Mum's favourite bowl.'

'You tell me I should talk about stuff and when I do, you change the fucking subject.'

Fee gets up and brings two cokes from the fridge. She rips one open and hands me it. 'Go ahead, I'm listening,' she says

I tell her about the light switch game, about how he would threaten to punish Mum if I broke the rules and put the light back on. How he'd bring a reward if I was good, then take it off me even if I hadn't done anything. She asks if he hit me.

'Sometimes, but he knew I wasn't afraid of that so it didn't happen much. But he made sure he hurt me in other ways. He made sure the me I could have been was never going to be. He destroyed that version.'

Fee asks me to stand up and turn around.

'He had no right to do what he did, but he can't do that to you now, because you've got a Sun God looking out for you.'

She traces the shape of my tattoo.

'That won't scare a man who's able to scare the sun away. You saw what happened when I mentioned his name, how it shrank, disappeared.'

She looks at me as if I'm mad. 'It was a cloud, a cloud passing over, that's all. How can anyone scare the sun?'

I take out two twenty pound notes from my wallet.

'I thought you understood, but don't worry, no one does.'

I put the notes on the table.

'That's for the bowl.'

She won't take it, says it was a few quid from a charity shop. 'You don't have to go home, you can stay if you want. Be nice to have some company.'

I can stay at Fee's for the next two nights, her Mum's definitely away until then. Fee hates that I sleep with the curtains open but apart from that we get on OK. It's so easy being around her. I don't even mind that the house is old and dark, keeps things cooler. There's a basement under the house and it's full of supplies – tinned food, longlife milk, tea, coffee, packs and packs of bottle water. Someone could hide away in here if they needed to.

It takes longer to get to work but every morning Fee texts me to make sure I got in OK, and when I get home we eat together and she asks how my day went. I tell her about Malik and she agrees he's a knob. I want to tell her so much more but I need to wait. Make sure.

Her Mum rings every night and each time Fee makes out like she doesn't want to talk to her, raises her eyebrows, says yes, no, will do, OK. I've been away from home for three nights now and Mum hasn't texted me once but Snoop Dog Sista's been in touch. She's still denying it was her snooping in my room. Even if it was me, I wouldn't say anything. You know that. I don't though, do I, Celine, because it would be your word against mine and guess who'd they'd believe? I should thank her. That was the start. That was my first heroic act. Stepping up to take the fall for her. I can see why it had to be now. These things are preparation. These things make us what we become.

There's only five days to the solstice. I thought about celebrating it with Fee. She's already mentioned it but what if the sun thinks we're not deserving. What if judgement has already been passed. What if June 21st isn't the longest day but the last one? The Mayans predicted the end of the world and everyone scoffed when it didn't happen. What if their calculations were wrong? What if mine are right?

Thursday, 16th June 2022

Didn't sleep very well last night. All the doubts, all the fears ambushed me soon as I lay my head down. When I woke up the worst of them was still there. Wouldn't go away. Still can't get rid. All the way in to work he hung around in my head, like some stupid fucking song. He's still there. Fee was wrong, forgiveness doesn't set you free. The damage is done and it won't ever heal.

'It's a hot one today, isn't it, love? They said we were going to get a nice warm summer, not too hot they said, but here it is again. Scorchio.'

It's a greenhouse on the top deck and the woman opposite me is sweating so much her face is on the move, her make-up melting like an ice cream.

She dabs at her forehead with a hanky. 'I never thought I'd moan about the heat, but they can shove it where the sun don't shine.'

My phone vibrates in my pocket. It's another update.

The burnt-out car found at the site of the fire has been identified as belonging to a Mr Robert Tate. Further updates to follow shortly.

They're closing in, just like he is. All my life I've been trying to dodge him. Keep him at a distance and now he wants to show up, spoil everything like he always does.

The bus route takes us past a school. It's a red brick one, iron railings. Looks just like my last junior school. Dad insisted on walking with me. It was my third one in as many years. Exclusions don't look good on a school record, Dad reminded me on the way.

I'm going to have a word with your teacher, make sure he keeps a good eye on you, before things get out of hand. As I walk with him I imagine the words he'll use. Sneaky, sly, snide. I even tried to lose him, ran into the mass that was herding into the building, thought I could get lost amongst all the other kids. But he was like a terrier, tracked me all the way. Followed me into class. Told the teacher what he needed to do and then before he left he announced I was a bed-wetter. Said it out loud, so all the class could hear. Humiliated me so I'd be broken goods from the start.

I can't concentrate at work, keep making mistakes, but Kojak's in a good mood and he doesn't say anything. Curtis not calling round has obviously been a good thing. We've got another mechanic in to cover Mo's absence. Malik's not particularly friendly to him, but to be honest, neither am I. I'm keeping my distance from both. Got too much to think about. I need to prepare for tonight. No idea what I'll walk in to. Mum might not let me in. Dad might already be at the house. She'll have been talking to him, giving him the lowdown about the BBQ. How I hit Celine. I shouldn't have done that. I'm not sure she did go snooping. I think it was me put the cuttings back in the wrong order. The last time I looked at them I panicked, stuffed them back inside. I'm getting too jumpy. This is what he does. This is what he makes me.

I text Celine and say I got it wrong. Say I'm sorry, that I'll see her later, apologise properly. She texts back that she's not at home. She's staying at her mate's, that Mum has told her to stay put. I ask if Dad's at the house. She says he's still up in Scotland with work.

I don't break for lunch, playing catch-up because of my errors.

'Has she gone all quiet on you?'

Malik's at my shoulder.

'You been on that phone all morning.'

'Heard anything from Mo?' I say.

Malik skulks off and I get back to checking the weather, then the news, then the weather again. Temps are on the up. That woman on the bus was right. They got it wrong. I don't trust them anyway. Their readings. Don't trust anyone's readings. I need to do some more tests. I need to make sure.

I get a text from Mum. She wants to know where I am, tells me to come home. We need to talk, she says.

I shout hello as I walk into the lounge. Mum's sitting at the dining table, half empty bottle by her elbow, full glass in her hand.

'Sit down. We need to talk.'

Mum pushes one of the dining chairs out from under the table with her foot.

'Before you say anything, I've already apologised to Celine. I was out of order for what I did and it won't happen again.'

'It was me found the cuttings, not Celine.'

She's tipsy and the drink is giving her bravado.

'I knew you were up to something. I knew you'd been up to your old tricks.'

'OK, I've got a box file of cuttings, so what?'

'They'll press charges this time, Luke. You're an adult now, responsible for your actions, they won't tiptoe around you anymore.'

I get up, tap the side of the bottle. 'You should treat yourself to something decent. You don't know what's in this,' I say.

'They come down heavy on people like you these days. They'll send you to prison.'

'People like me? All I've done is keep some press cuttings about some fires. That's not a crime last time I checked. I've got an interest in fires, so what? I could be in training to be a firespotter for all they know.'

Mum plays with the stem of her glass, chinks her fingernails against it.

'When we moved to London it was supposed to be a fresh start, that's why we came. I gave up everything, my home, my husband, my friends, all because of you, because you promised you'd stop if we left.'

I sit back in the chair, fold my arms.

'We could go together. If you hand yourself in they might go easy. They'll see you need help. They can look into your school reports, the therapist you saw, they'll have records. All they have to do is take a look at your room, all those posters, all that mess on the wall. Can't you see that's not right? Something's really wrong, Luke.'

Something is wrong. But it's not me.

'Is he here? Is Dad going to make an entrance? Are we going have a fanfare?'

'A man is *missing*, Luke. You need to go to the police, you have to! This has gone too far!'

'I can't do that, Mum.'

'If you won't do it then I'll have to do it.'

'Go ahead. Like I say, there's some newspaper cuttings in my room, I've an interest in fires – not exactly forensic proof, is it? Why don't we wait for Dad to come down? Have a proper discussion about it. You owe me that at least. You knew what he was like, you knew what he was doing and you didn't say anything, so my guess it, this is all bluff. You won't go to the police because you haven't got the guts.'

She looks like she does after a late shift, like she always did when he was around. Worn out, tired. I pick up the bottle from the table, fill her glass up. Keep pouring until a cushion of gin sits on the top. It clings to the rim. One more drop, that's all it would take.

I place the bottle back down and Mum picks up her handbag from the floor. She reaches inside and brings out an envelope.

'There's five hundred pounds in there. Pack your things and get out. I never want to see you again.'

She pushes the envelope across the table towards me.

'And you were always going to choose him, weren't you? Ever thought about how that made me feel? You choosing not to believe me. You always took his side. You took everyone's side but mine. I was such a bad boy. You need to know something. That empty house, the one that caught fire.'

The ping of a text sounds on Mum's phone. It's face down on the table near Mum but my reflexes are quicker. I read the text.

– THX FOR GIVING ME ANOTHER CHANCE. DON'T WORRY ABOUT LUKE I'LL DEAL WITH HIM. GETTING TRAIN TUESDAY ETA 8.40 XX

The way he's used capitals, it's like he's right here using his big shouty voice to deliver his warnings. I feel the warmth in my trouser leg. He can still make me piss myself after all these years. He can still do it.

'Don't worry about Luke, I'll deal with him. Deal with him! *Deal with him!*'

I shout it as loud as he would and Mum flees, just like she used to. I grab the half-empty bottle. Mum can cover some ground when she needs to but my legs are longer. As she nears the lounge door I lift my arm, swing the bottle like a baseball bat. There's a dull thud as it hits the base of her skull. She doesn't scream, she doesn't make a sound, she just stops, like she's run into an invisible wall. I wait for her to turn around, blast me, give me what for, but there's nothing to give anymore. She drops, like a bird, and I catch her in my arms.

It's like the bench was made for her, it's the perfect length, the perfect width. I cross Mum's arms over her chest, tuck her hands in under her armpits. The shed window casts a square of sunlight across her and she looks so peaceful, and so young. All the pain is gone from her face.

I smooth her hair and kiss her forehead.

'I couldn't risk it, you know what he's like, Mum. He would have messed things up like he always does. I need to go sort something and I can't let anything get in the way. I thought I had sorted it, but you know me. But this time I will.'

I take the apples on the window ledge, place them at Mum's head and feet, then hold up my arms.

'Please accept this offering as proof that I need no further test. Please take this gift and know there is no price too high, no cost too great, to make up for how we have failed you. I will answer any calling. Whatever it takes I am not afraid.'

I lock the shed, tuck the key into my jeans pocket. I pack some things into my rucksack and pick up Mum's phone and purse. I pick the glass up from the table. There's a mark on the rim, Mum's lipstick, in the shape of her smile.

It's nearly half six and the front door of the garage is locked and the blinds are down. I take the corner into the side street, grab a wheelie bin from the front garden of a house opposite. I wheel it against the back gate, climb onto it and check the yard out before I jump.

I walk over to the back room window, use my knife to chip away at the putty. Bits have already broken off and it doesn't take long to prise the pane away and squeeze myself through. The window's not alarmed. It doesn't shut properly and it was always triggering it so Kojak took it off. Once I'm inside I disable all the alarms and then go straight into Kojak's office. I take the map off the wall and key in the code. I pray that Kojak hasn't changed it as I pull the handle. It opens.

I sit in the café with an iced tea and do a search. Who'd have thought this craggy little island would have so many. Find nearly two hundred. Most have been abandoned, but not all. The third one I ring I get lucky. They've had a cancellation that very morning. I read out the long number on the back of Mum's credit card and it's done, booked. I say I won't be arriving till late and she tells me she'll leave the key under the doormat if it's after midnight.

Fee's sent me four texts.

– *Just checking you got home OK.*
– *You said you'd text* ☹
– *You know I'm here for you.*
– *Love you XXXXXXXXXX*

As I read the last one, she sends me another.

– *Text me you moron!! I'm getting worried. XXX*

I ring her and she has a go at me for not texting.

'You never ever text, you say you will but you never do. Listen, there's something I need to tell you, I was going to tell you before but I wasn't sure.'

'Let's go away. My treat. Let's go away for a few days and celebrate the solstice.'

'When?'

'Now.'

She's all shocked, surprised.

'Meet me at Paddington Station in an hour.'

The station's hectic, thick with people coming and going, but as soon as I see her, everything stills.

'Sorry I'm so late.'

'I wasn't sure if you'd come.'

She steps forward and gives me a hug. 'Miss out on a free trip, you kidding me?' She raises her mouth to me. I know I should kiss her. I know that's what I should do but I can't. There's a rank taste in my mouth. I drank a litre of water but it won't go.

I tell her I've got the tickets already. She wants to know where we're going but I say it won't be a surprise if I do that. She wants to get some mints. There's a stand at the entrance to the newsagents. It would have been displaying newspapers and magazines but now it's home to a range of sun-blocks, moisturisers and cheap plastic visors. The newspapers sit in two separate piles by the till. I pick one up, flick through it. There's a small piece on the fire on page five. That's a good sign. No mention of a body, just the car. I check out each page. There's three more articles on fires. They're all being blamed on the high temperatures. *Global warming is turning the UK into a fire hazard,* says a Minister. *The acceleration in global warming is an international crisis,* says another. *We must unite and look towards a common goal to win this battle.*

The bloke at the till coughs. It's code for stop reading the fucking paper. I close it and put it back.

'You going to tell me where we're going?' Fee says, popping a mint into her mouth. 'All you said was to pack for the beach, but is this a UK beach or a French beach? Are you whisking me away to foreign parts?'

'I'm not telling, it will spoil the surprise,' I say.

'Are we going North or South, East or West? Come on, just one clue.'

I check the forecast on my phone, read it out. 'Clear skies with plenty of sunshine. Temperatures will rise slightly but will stay around the mid to high thirties for the next few days. No solar alerts predicted.'

'Good. Don't want to get there and have to stay inside the whole time. On second thoughts…' She squeezes my arm. 'That might not be such a bad thing.'

Our train gets announced. The 20:45 to Bristol Temple Meads is due to depart in seven minutes. I grab Fee's arm and we run through the station and board the train with only two minutes to go. We look out the window, watch everything slide past. The tracks, cables, signals soon give way to concrete blocks and tall buildings. There's a lot of green glass. All the buildings seem to be made of the same coloured glass. Not a great building material for birds but they're great for me. I can soon fill a rucksack with dead pigeons if I go scavenging up town.

Fee falls asleep about half an hour after we leave. It's the rocking of the train. I wish it would relax me as easy.

'Tickets please.'

I hand the ticket inspector our tickets. She checks them and tells me to enjoy my journey. There's something about her that reminds me of Mum. It's not the uniform, it's her voice. She's got the same bloody voice. Got that same polite weariness. She flicks me a quick smile and moves on and I relax back in my seat, let the motion of the train do its job.

I can't sleep. Keep thinking about Mum. I know I have to try and blank that. What's done is done. I can't go back in time, undo it.

Some things you can't undo but some things you can change, some things you can alter.

Fee stays asleep for a good hour. When she wakes she sticks on her headphones. Listens to music. I'm hungry, haven't eaten since lunchtime. I ask her if she wants anything.

She shakes her head and I head off to find the snack bar. It's right at the other end of the train but there aren't many carriages and there aren't many passengers. I scroll through my contacts and block Kojak. When he opens up tomorrow he's not going to be at all happy and I don't want to hear.

The snack bar hasn't got much left. I buy an egg sandwich and a Fanta. Fee's got her headphones slung round her neck when I get back.

'You going to tell me where we're going, or is it still a big secret?'

'It's somewhere you've always wanted to go to.'

'Sweden?'

I try and think of when she's ever mentioned Sweden. What conversation that was.

'Kidding. It's OK, I'm guessing it's the West Country, seeing as the train is going that way. I can hold my curiosity for a little longer.'

She sticks her headphones back in her ears and I look at the striped sky, at the shocking pink melting into the deep blue. We take so much for granted. So much that is there, on offer every day, every night. It never stops working and we can't pay it a little respect. No wonder it gets angry, no wonder it wants revenge.

It's twenty to eleven when we pull into Bristol. The station's nearly empty, I count three other people, apart from us. In London there's more night time traffic than ever. Buses, trains, tubes, they run right through, because people go out later and stay out later. Too hot to party too early. We are finally becoming more like Europe, as most of Europe is becoming more like a desert.

Outside a group of black cabs sit ticking like cockroaches. One pulls away, crawls towards us and we get in. As it moves off we slide around on the seats. I tell Fee to hold onto the hand rail. The streetlights disappear as we head out the city to the coast. It's only an hour's drive away. There's nothing to see out of the windows, and we're both too tired to talk, so we doze.

The cab drops off the main roads, takes smaller and smaller lanes with fewer and fewer houses, then suddenly comes to stop in the middle of nowhere. I pay and the cabbie points to a path. His satnav is saying we should follow it to the end. We grab our bags, and I use my phone to light the way. My trainers make a crunching sound on the gravel and Fee shouts for me to slow down. I want to tell her that's not how it works. It's an uphill climb and if we slow we'll lose rhythm, lose momentum. The path bears right and leads to a gate labelled Keeper's Cottage.

I open the gate. Solar lights line the path up to the cottage. There's another light over the front door but the rest of the cottage is in darkness. We dump our bags on the step and ring the doorbell. The door is opened by a woman with short grey hair wearing a short grey dressing gown.

'Heard the taxi, thought it must be you,' she says. Her West Country accent makes her sound like she's pleased to see us, like she knows us.

'I'm Martha, the landlady. You'll meet my husband Tom in the mornin'. He'll be over to do the official business, health and safety, rules and regs. That kind of thing. I won't keep you as I know you've come a long way an' you'll be wanting your bed. Oh dear, someone's tired!'

Fee is yawning. Martha hands me a set of keys. 'You'll find tea and coffee and other essentials in the kitchen, and there's sandwiches in the fridge in case you're hungry. Here, take this, you'll need it. Just follow the path round and you'll drop down to the causeway. Not far, only take you a few minutes.'

She hands me a heavy black torch. 'You'll see the lighthouse at the end of it. The air conditioning takes pound coins but we always give guests a heads up, so you shouldn't need to top up till morning'. If you need any change have a word with hubby in the morning, he'll call by after breakfast. He can be a bit officious so don't take no notice. You'll find sitting room and kitchen on the first floor, bedroom and bathroom on second. Top floor is a viewing platform-cum-chill area. It's the old lantern room. There's information about the history of the lighthouse and Tom can fill you in with anything else tomorrow. He likes to think of himself as a lighthouse keeper, even though he's never been one! So just play along, keep him 'appy. Sorry we still got water restrictions out here, so if you can take a shower instead of a bath that would be much appreciated. Mind, you got the sea right on your doorstep, that's a big enough bath for anybody.'

She wishes us a good night and shuts the door. I like it when people do that, say what they need to and then that's it done. No awkward moments, no weird silences.

'Did she say lighthouse keeper? Is that it, is that the surprise?' Fee asks, wide-eyed and wide awake.

I switch on the torch. A wedge of light bleaches the path, turns the mucky grey gravel brilliant white.

'Let's see, shall we,' I say, waving the torch about, lighting up the shrubbery.

'Come on then, let's find this house of light. Can't be too hard to find. Aren't they supposed to shine out for lost souls?'

We follow the path. It curves and dips as it slopes away and the shrubbery disappears, and there it is. The house of light, the home for lost souls. For a lighthouse, it's quite short and squat but it still stops us in our tracks. It's at the end of a short causeway. Floodlit from below it stands out like an exclamation mark at the end of a sentence.

'Race you!' Fee says. I let her run off. Want to stay put, want to imagine the viewing platform. Me watching the sun come up. How good that will be. How great a spot have I picked. Can't wait to get set up, do some tests, check the results.

Fee's waiting by the door. I wave the torch above her head and we look up to the top of the lighthouse.

'It's nearly as tall as you,' Fee says.

I open the door, find the light switch, and Fee pushes past me. As she runs up the stairs I tell her to be careful.

'Shut it, grandad,' she shouts back.

The steps are narrow and seem to twist round and round forever. Fee's found the lounge. I dump my rucksack and fall onto the sofa and five minutes later Fee appears with sandwiches and drinks from the fridge.

'That was very kind of Martha to think about our stomachs, and it was very kind of you to bring me to my favourite place in all the world.' She kisses me on the cheek. 'It's the best thing anyone has ever done for me.'

We sit on the floor and stuff our faces. Fee lets out a long low burp and rubs her belly and warns me that she might pop a fart next. I beat her to it.

She wants to explore but I tell her it's best we get our heads down and check out the lighthouse in the morning.

'But it is morning,' she says. 'It's gone midnight.'

The food has given me an energy boost so I say OK, and we climb the spiral staircase that leads to the viewing gallery above.

The room is full of lights. Solar powered, they give off a soft pale light. Some are blue and some are pink and they are scattered around the floor, between giant beanbags and giant cushions.

Fee throws herself down onto a beanbag. I sit down beside her on a cushion. There's a clear sky and it's a big low moon. I can handle this. This kind of dark. Moonshine and stars, solar lights and Fee.

The main lens that would have lit the sea has been removed but there are photographs of when it was in action on one of the coffee tables. I show Fee but she's not that bothered. Too busy looking through the glass ceiling.

'I've got a top like that, all shimmery and sparkly.'

I look up, try and imagine her wrapped in a patch of the night sky.

'Did you bring it with you?'

'It's a black lurex boob-tube. A going-out top, for when I want to pull. I don't need to do that now, do I?'

I turn to face her. 'But I want you to,' I whisper.

'Pull other guys?'

'Not other guys, me. I'd like to see you dress up for me.'

'I thought you liked it when I undress for you.' We make out under the stars.

After a bit I get up and walk over to the window. At night there's no telling where the horizon is, no telling where the sea meets the sky. You don't get nights like this in London. Nights so dark you don't know which way is up.

'Shit, I've got déjà vu. I know exactly what I'm going to say and I know exactly what I'm going to do.'

She holds out her hand for me to help her to her feet. I yank her up and we both stand, faces pressed close to the glass, looking at the darkness.

'Do you think there could be another of us out there, another Luke and Fee looking at the exact same sky but in another world?'

'You are on another planet,' I say.

'I'd forgive you anything, you know that, don't you.'

I get panicked wondering why she's talking like this, like she knows what's happened. Like she knows why we're here.

'I'm lost. I'm lost in Fee space,' I say. 'You need to give me a clue because you're not making any sense.'

Fee sits down on the bench that runs beneath the windows and

I sit down next to her. We look out at the hillside pinpricked with light from the houses.

'Look like fallen stars, don't they, Fee says. 'The house lights. Do you think they're happy, the people inside? The mums and dads, the kids? Do you think they're living happy lives?'

'Who knows what goes on behind closed doors,' I say and regret it.

'Do you want a house like that, a family?'

I say I haven't really thought about it and she shifts. It's the tiniest movement away from me.

'There's a lot to do before that,' I say.

'Is there?'

I lay my hand on her shoulder, ask if she's OK. She shrugs it off.

'I knew I should have stayed in London, knew I shouldn't have come here with you.'

I try and work out what it is I've done or said.

'I was going to tell you when you stayed but I bottled it.'

'Tell me what?'

'I'm pregnant.'

I must have thumped the window, because there's a mark on the pane. I wish I hadn't and I wish I hadn't sworn but I did and Fee had the same look on her face that Celine did and I want to hold her and tell I'm sorry. I reach out but she's already at the stairs. Hear her footsteps ring out on the metal steps. Tip tap, tip tap, tip tap.

She pauses and there's a panicked stumbling before she falls.

I find her at the bottom of the stairs, in a twisted heap. She sits up and I see that her above her right knee the skin has split and blood is welling. I kneel down next to her, ask her if she's OK. She nods but she's white as the walls and shaky as fuck. I tell her to put her arm around my neck and help her to the sofa.

'I'll get something to stop the bleeding,' I say. 'Keep pressing on it.'

I find the bathroom and soak a flannel. The blood's running down her leg now. I clean her leg. Feel an idiot, a dick. All that chit chat about the houses and the families.

'I'm sorry. I wanted to tell you before, I did, and I kept thinking I'd come on, that I was just late but I'm always on time. To the second.'

I press the flannel to her knee to stop the bleeding.

'Don't go all mute on me.'

She's doing that silent crying, where the tears creep out and slide down your face, you can wipe them away, pretend it's not happening. I take my hand away from her leg. The bleeding hasn't stopped but it's just oozing now.

'You should run it under the shower, keep the wound clean. I'll see if there's a first aid kit somewhere.'

'I said I think I'm pregnant, so say something!'

'Are you sure?'

It's the wrong thing to say. Fee blasts me. She thinks I'm trying to pass the buck, make out it's not mine, make out she's a slapper, make out she doesn't know how to read a pregnancy test, make out she can't use contraception. It's a knife attack with words. I can't dodge all of them and I end up throwing a few of my own.

'You fell pregnant the first time we did it? How can I go from being a virgin to a Dad in two weeks? How come I let you talk me into not using anything? You might be late, there's a first time for everything.'

'I've done the test. Twice. Believe me I didn't want it to be positive.'

Blood's running down her leg. It's going to mark the sofa and spill on to the floor. I tell her she should take a bath but she just wants a plaster.

'It needs cleaning properly, you'd be better soaking it, and you're going to have a nice bruise tomorrow. It's brewing already.'

'Why don't you go for a walk,' she says. 'I can sort myself out. Just leave me alone.'

'I don't want to go for a walk. You've just fallen down the stairs and cut yourself, I want to make sure you're OK.'

'Luke, I want to be on my own, you've got a torch, Martha gave you one.'

'I'm not going out to wander on a beach in the middle of the fucking night.'

'Well just go and sit on the fucking step.'

I insist on running her bath and helping her into it and she lets me, then I slam the lighthouse door behind me. How can I tell her the shithead of a bloke that managed to get her pregnant doesn't want to go for a walk because he's scared, because after all these years, after all this time, he's still scared of the dark. I've seen the way guys check her out, the way they slip me a look as if to say, how did *you* manage that? If they knew I still needed a night light on, still woke up in a piss-soaked bed from time to time, they'd be in there, hitting on her so hard.

I switch the torch on. It's a full moon but sand at night isn't easy. A clump of dune catches me out and I end up on all fours, stalks of dry grass poke into me and I decide to sit where I've fallen.

I think about a life growing inside her. Think about her belly getting bigger, rounder. Think about her as a Mum, me as a Dad. We'd be a family, I'd have my own family, one I wanted. Maybe this is my future, this is my reward. I stand up, cup my hands to my mouth.

'I'm going to be a father. I'm going to be a Dad. And not just any Dad, the best fucking Dad. Did you hear that?'

The darkness sucks it from my tongue. I shout it, louder. Loud as I can. Want the sea to know, want the moon to know, want the sun to know, want the whole fucking universe to know. Maybe she's right, and there is a parallel universe with another her, another me. I wonder what he's doing right now, what he's done. Wonder if he's got someone like Fee, wonder if he's got a family. Wonder if he knows how to stop his sun from dying. Wonder if he knows how much he is willing to sacrifice.

I watch the light on the water. The light that's come from the sun, by way of the moon. It trickles down the sea towards me, carried on the wave like a pulse, like a heartbeat.

Friday, 17th June 2022

Fee's stretched out on the sofa in her bra and pants and I can see the full size of her bruise. It's the size of Ireland.

'Wow, that must hurt,' I say.

'That's why I slept in here, didn't want you knocking into me in your sleep.'

'Nothing to do with the curtains being open?'

'I honestly don't know how you can sleep like that, I have to have blackouts. It obviously doesn't bother you, you've slept through the whole morning.'

I ask if she wants breakfast.

'Had mine hours ago. It's nearly lunchtime.'

Fee's watching a sitcom on the telly and the same canned laughter happens every ten seconds.

'Tom came over earlier, said it's more relaxed out here. No patrols or curfews. Said we can do pretty much as we want, within reason.'

'Did you let him in dressed like that?'

'No, I wore a t-shirt. He dropped off the house rules, you can read them while I shower.'

I can't help but check out her belly as she walks by. It doesn't look any different, she doesn't look any different.

I read the rules as I make myself some toast.

Please leave the place as you find it.

No uninvited guests.

No loud music after 10pm.

Vacate by 10am on leaving day.
Any damages must be paid for.
Some essentials eg milk/coffee/tea provided.
Takeaway menus by phone.

There's a small paragraph about the history of the lighthouse and the surrounds. It says there's another beach the other side of the headland, it's smaller but there's cliffs and rock-pools.

I take my toast into the bedroom, stand by the window and look out along the main beach. A wide belt of white sand runs alongside a blue sparkling sea. Postcard pretty it is but I'm betting the other beach is a lot more interesting.

I eat half a slice of toast and then lay it on the bedside table. Fee's clothes are all over the floor. I pick them up, lay them over the arm of a wicker chair. It's white, the same colour as the walls, the same colour as the floor. I run my hands over the wall above the bed. I like the unevenness of the plaster, the roughness, and I like the way the lumps and bumps throw small shadows. I'm trying to figure out whether one of the shadows looks like a cat or not, when a shape straight out of Gotham City appears. A bat shape hangs above the cat shape. As I stare at it, it moves, rushes towards the ceiling and the caw of a seagull spins me round. A scrawny-looking gull is outside the window. Hovering mid-air, its beak prised open to show off the bright red gizzard. It's spied the toast. I pick up the half-eaten slice and chuck it out the window. It catches it in its beak, throws its head and shakes it down in one.

It hangs around for more. Scavengers. Vermin. Lowlife. Take a small baby if they could, was what Mum used to say. We went to Whitby one bank holiday, and Celine's fish and chips got taken straight out of her hands. I liked watching them do their flypasts, like bomber pilots. Deadly when they clocked a target. I'd copy them, go hunting for leftovers myself. Any litter that might combust. I'd tell Mum I was off to find a bin to dump it in and I'd find a spot away from the crowds, take out my magnifying glass and see what burnt quickest. Set fire to a cardboard box once, bits of it broke away, took flight. Flames were flying in the air. It felt good being in control, making something happen.

The gull drops so fast I feel sure it's going to hit the sea, become a bloody mess of beak and feathers. It knows just when to slow down, just when to drop down its feet. Lands gentle as feather, sits there bobbing up and down in all that sea. There aren't any others. Never seen that before. Never seen a lone gull. Least there's no competition.

I know it'll be there. I know I don't need to check but I can't stop myself. I crawl under the bed, pull the rucksack towards me and open it up. I take out one of the bundles. Hadn't noticed how new they looked, how new they smelt, how new they felt.

'Luke.'

My head hits the bed frame as I reverse out. Fee's in the doorway, a beach towel rolled up under her arm.

'Fancy a swim?'

She's got on the craziest sun suit and beach socks.

'Acid green's your colour,' I say.

'Shut up, Mr Boring.'

I grab the parasol by the door. 'We won't need that, there aren't any patrols out here,' Fee says.

'We still need to be careful. It's in the thirties.'

'Well, you can carry it.'

She runs across the sand and I drop the parasol and run after her.

The tide's so far out the sea's hardly visible. No more than a thick blue line.

'The sea's fallen off the edge,' Fee shouts.

'Watch you don't,' I shout back.

We run for a good three minutes and then it's just there, as if it's been hiding. I throw my flip flops back up the beach and run through the warm shallows. Slugs of wet sand squeeze through our toes, splatter the backs of our legs.

'No splashing,' Fee says, as she kicks a wall of spray over me. I kick one back and dive in. It's not deep enough and my nose scrapes along the bottom. I wade further out, keep wading until the water is chest height.

'It's like swimming in the biggest bath ever,' Fee says.

Fee floats on her back and I take off. Some people don't get it, think swimming is boring, repetitive. That's what I liked about it. Swam a lot when I was a kid. Used to go to the local pool. The rhythm helped clear my head, helped me focus. Did length after length. Swam until the tips of my fingers went all wrinkly. One time the chlorine was so strong I couldn't see. It blinded me. Had to feel my way home. I was clinging to the walls of buildings, trying to plan out the route from memory. My worst fear, the dark, and I go and plunge myself into it,

Not sure how long I've been swimming for when I hear her. Have to tread water, squint to see where she is, because the sunlight hitting the sea is doing its best to hide her. She's at the shoreline, hands cupped around her mouth, shouting my name. I've swum further than I thought. She sounds scared and I wonder if something's wrong, wonder if her fall down the stairs hurt her more than she said it did. I wave at her and she wakes back. When I reach her, she flings her arms around my neck.

'I didn't think you were coming back.' Her lashes are all clumped together in big brown spikes and her eyes look as sad as they did last night. 'I thought you weren't going to stop, thought you were going to keep going, leave me.'

I hold her until she calms down then offer to give her a piggy-back. She's not heavy but it's a decent hike back up the beach. I play a trick, tell myself I'm on exercises, carrying a backpack full of supplies. The trick is to keep moving, if you come to a halt you've had it.

I set the parasol up. We strip our wet things off, sit underneath it and Fee asks me to dry her hair. I'm too rough with the towel and I turn her hair into a giant fuzz ball.

She shakes her head from side to side and it doesn't budge. She looks like a retro porn star. I tell her that and she pulls me towards her. She wants to have sex but it feels wrong.

'It won't harm the baby, if that's what you're worried about. You can do it until you pop.'

'It doesn't feel right somehow.'

'Luke, it doesn't know, it's not watching us. It's only a few cells at the minute, that's all it is.'

She cocks her head to one side. 'Is something bothering you? You were shouting in your sleep last night, could hear you from the lounge. Sounded like you having a nightmare?'

She sits up, stretches her legs out in front of her, then folds herself over them, easy as a gymnast. 'Why do you need forgiveness?'

My brain screeches through gears so fast.

'You've been a bit weird since we met up. I don't mean like weird, weird. You just don't seem your normal self. Stuff at home still not right?'

'It was you. I was asking forgiveness from you,' I say.

She buys it.

'Soon as we had sex you dumped me, thought it was because I'd done something wrong. That must have been playing on my mind.'

'I'm sorry. That wasn't very nice of me to push you away, but I do that. I do that a lot. But you don't need to ask forgiveness, you did nothing wrong, OK?"

I say her big hair makes her look like a flower, a dandelion. She laughs and then as if to prove my point a wasp buzzes round her head. I tell her not to move and she does the opposite, jumps around and throws her head about and the wasp buzzes about her face. She screams, flicks it away with her hand and runs around in circles. It won't leave here, sticks right by her and then she's into wasp-hating mode. Screaming and yelling.

'That's not helping,' I say. 'You're making it angry.'

'Get rid of it, just get rid of it.'

I tell her to stand still, stay calm. 'It'll get bored and go away if you stop moving.'

There's a scream straight out of *Psycho*. 'It's in my hair. It's in my fucking hair!'

'I see it,' I say.

Wings tucked back, balanced on a single strand, it takes awkward little steps, deeper into her frizz ball.

'Please *do* something!'

I wrap one of the towels around my hands, tell her to stay very still. Keep my eyes fixed on the tiny tightrope walker. I need to time it right, might only get once chance. I slam my fists together, press them against each other hard as I can. Fee whines that I'm pulling at her hair.

'You want me to get it out, you want me to kill it, don't you?'

I withdraw my hands, inspect the damage. The smart stripes, the neat wings are no more.

'It's a hornet, not a wasp.' I show her the broken body and she knocks the towel out of my hands as if it could spring back to life, sting her. 'It's dead, it can't harm you.'

'You didn't have to shove it in my face and you didn't have to pull my hair like that, it bloody hurt.'

'Good,' I say. It feels right it should hurt. Feels right she should be in pain. 'How you can be so scared of something that small?'

'Don't you dare go there, Mr Scared of the Fucking Dark. I'm hungry, I want to eat, you coming?'

She walks away, naked except for her acid green socks and mad as fuck hair.

'Hey, you need to cover up,' I say.

'There are no rules out here.'

'The sun's still dangerous.'

I throw her towel at her. It hits her back, falls onto the sand. It's not about rules, it's about respect. She carries on, tells me to hurry up.

I pick up the towel with the broken remains, hold it high above my head.

You are the giver of life
All life is from you
And all life is equal
May all life return to you.

Saturday, 18th June 2022

People shouldn't have to share a bed together, just because you're a couple it doesn't mean you should have to give up your sleep. Fee came in to bed last night and I ended up decamping to the sofa. She wanted the curtains closed and she wanted the fan on all night. That was one of her first whinges, the fact there wasn't any air con. It shouldn't be allowed, should be compulsory, she said. I reminded her out here the rules don't apply.

In the summer, I love to be woken by the sun. In winter, it feels wrong to be woken by an alarm. Hate waking before day's arrived, hate having to wake when night is still here.

The sun wakes me before six. Fee's still out of it, which is good because I can set off early and do a recce before she wakes. Tom's left rules and Martha's left beach bags. I pack a few supplies into one of the bags and head for the main beach. Want to investigate the dunes. There's a lot of beach and a lot of dunes but not much to forage. A chewed stick left by a dog walker, an empty tube of sun cream, four paper cups, some scrappy bits of ice lolly wrappings and one small paper bag.

This time in the morning it's hard to imagine how threatening the sun can get, will get. I check the stats. Today's is a degree higher than yesterday, but the forecasters said it would rise by that much. It does look like things have stabilised since Thursday. My last offering seems to have been acceptable.

I want to check out the other bay, the smaller one. I climb over the rocky outcrop that separates the two beaches. This one is a lot smaller but it's wilder, rockier, so there'll be more chance of flotsam and jetsam. Me and Celine had rabbits called that. Hers was Flotsam, mine was Jetsam. Of course Dad had to point out they were named after rubbish, washed-up dregs.

Most of this beach is roped off because it butts up to some seriously crumbling cliffs, and there's evidence of a recent landslip. Big boulders of earth sit behind the rope, leaking sludge-grey tide marks into the sand.

I step over the rope. Bits of trees - branches, stumps, even whole bushes - lie at the foot of the cliffs. Some have still got soil clinging to the roots. I head for the older falls, the dead wood, the dried-out branches. Stick as much as I can into the bag.

There are lots of rock pools and they've gathered a decent crop of mussels. We could eat them tonight. I could build a small fire on the beach and cook them. We could spend the night there. It should be cooler. If the air is warmer than the sea it can pick up moisture, get a chance to dampen, lose some heat.

I watch a gull do just that, wings stretched wide it cools itself off by skimming the surface. Cruises like that for a while, then does a near vertical take-off, fighter jet style. It wheels up and up until all that's left is a tiny speck.

I wonder if it's the same gull I saw at the window. Snapshots flick through my head. Me chucking the toast. The gull swallowing it. Dropping out of view. Then me diving under the bed. Opening the rucksack. Taking out the money. I try and see the shot where I'm putting the money back, but I can't. I can't see that because it didn't happen.

I take the lighthouse steps three at a time. Push myself up and off the cold walls. There's a film fast-forwarding in my head. Fee in the bedroom. Her looking under the bed, pulling out the rucksack, finding the money.

I carry on up the stairs to the bedroom. The rucksack is as I left it. Mouth wide open, money spewing out. I shove the notes back inside, zip it shut and get changed.

Fee's sitting watching TV in the lounge.

'I'm going back to the other beach, there's mussels,' I say. 'Thought I could build a small fire and we could eat them on the beach later.'

'Why you wearing a dress?'

I tell her it's not a dress. 'It's a knee-length hoodie, the material's got built-in sun protection. You should get yourself some protective wear.'

'Not really my style.'

She tells me to stick my shades on and put my hood up.

'Suppose it's cool in a druid kind of way. Come on then, let's go.'

She stands up, wants one of the buckets.

I tell her about the rockpools. Says she might slip, hurt herself even more. 'Most of the beach has been roped off because of landslides. It's too dangerous.'

'I like a bit of danger. Surely you know that by now.'

'I won't be long, be back for lunch.'

'You're avoiding me, you have been since we got here. Before I even mentioned the baby. What it is, Luke? Why don't you talk to me, tell me what's on your mind?'

'I need to do more tests. Should have done them already.'

'And you don't want me around, getting in the way. Is that it?'

'They have to be done properly.'

'You said you'd show me. You said the next time you did your tests you'd show me.'

'Tomorrow. I promise we'll do some together tomorrow.'

The rock pools are teeming with life. Spider crabs, mussels, limpets. I dip my finger into one, wiggle a few weeds about. A small see-through fish darts into view as a spider crab crawls out from under a stone, turning the water cloudy as it disturbs the sand at the bottom. I check out a few more. I'm on the lookout for a sea scorpion but I find something much better.

I scoop a baby starfish out. It sits on my fingertip, waving, its arms no more than buds. It's waving because it wants to go back where it came from. Likes the wet, not the dry. Don't want to distress it so I pop it back. It floats off my finger and settles under a sea fern. The temperature of the rock pool is over warm. A few more degrees and it won't survive, none of them will.

When I finish collecting mussels the sun is directly overhead. I find a twig and snap it in half, use my knife to pare one end to a sharp point and draw a large circle in the sand with it. It makes a very good pencil and the sand makes an excellent canvas. I ring the circle with triangular shapes and then add more shapes, more detail until I've replicated my Sun God tattoo.

I use the mussels from the red bucket, arrange them in the centre. The sun rays give the blue-black shells a rainbow sheen. The offerings may be small, but they are not without beauty.

Whatever you want, I am your servant.
Whatever you need, I will deliver.
Whatever it takes, I will do.

I refill the bucket, head back. Fee's sitting on the steps of the lighthouse, playing a game on her phone.

'Yay, the hunter returns.' She peers into the buckets, asks how many I collected.

'Enough for two,' I say.

'Ah, slight problemo. Shellfish and pregnancy, big no-no, so you can have them all. I'll get a takeaway. Speaking of food, lunch awaits.' She jumps up. 'I found some chutney, made a ploughman's.'

Happy Fee is back, and I wonder if food always makes her happy or whether being pregnant has given her an appetite. Some days I forget to eat. When I'm out on a scavenge or doing tests I can go all day without food.

We sit at the small counter separating the lounge from the kitchen to eat. Fee wants to know why the lighthouse doesn't get that hot.

'I thought it would, because it hasn't got air con, but it's not too bad.'

I tell her it doesn't have many windows and the outside is painted white. 'That all helps.'

'We should paint our houses white to reflect the sun rays.'

'We should,' I say.

'You're a little bit obsessed with the sun, aren't you? All those posters in your room, all the tests you do.'

'Everyone has a hobby.'

'But you're not a fan of it, are you? You don't seem to enjoy being in it.'

'I am its biggest fan. I just show it differently.'

'Will you show me one of your tests? When you next do one, take me with. I'd like to see.'

'Sure.'

I finish eating and take my plate over to the sink. Fee wants to give me a massage to get rid of my tension. It's a good release, she says. That would be lovely, I say.

'We could watch your favourite sitcom afterwards, if you want.'

It's such a simple thing but she's so fucking grateful, so fucking happy.

Fee needs to get the gallery ready and that gives me an opportunity to check on the temps. All channels report a sudden unexpected rise. It's back to being over forty degrees in London, and predictions are could continue to climb into the high forties and beyond. But the UK is lucky. It's still sitting in the orange area, the outer rim of a very unhealthy very red-looking area, which stretches around the globe in a thick band. Takes in continents, never mind countries, and the temperatures are hitting fifty degrees regularly and more. If there's a need for another offering, I'll have no option.

'Luke, I'm ready,' Fee calls.

She's good at massage. Doesn't hold back. I tell her she's got strong hands and she says all the better to beat you with and karate chops my back. She works on my shoulders and head and it does make me feel better. And we feel better for it. We cuddle up on the sofa and watch re-runs of an American TV show. Everything about it is brash and loud but Fee likes it. Two and a half hours later she finally gets bored, suggests we decamp to the beach.

'You can ring Martha and place our order,' she says. 'I know it's early but I'm hungry.'

I tell her she's always hungry.

I read out the order from a leaflet with a fiery red dragon on the front. Fee wants chicken chow mein. I order sweet and sour pork and a coke. Martha says she'll ring when the food arrives. Be here within the hour.

I pack a coolbox and pack some of the kindling I collected into the beach bag. I carry the box, the bag, the parasol and our beach towels. Fee brings the mussels. She wants to sit in our usual spot. I tell her to walk on a bit further, but she won't go too far in case she needs the loo.

'That's what sand dunes are for,' I say.

'I'm not a heathen like you,' she says. 'Here, this will do.'

I stick the parasol into the sand and lay the towels underneath it.

'I'm not sitting in the shade. It's half past five, there's no need for a sun brolly.'

'There's every need,' I say. 'It's getting hot again. They got it wrong.'

'Aren't you only supposed to eat mussels if there's an 'R' in the month?' Fee sticks her nose inside the buckets. 'Or is that oysters?'

Her face is glowing. I tell her she's caught the sun.

'Good. I don't want to be whitey-white.'

'You're fair skinned, you need to be careful.'

'You're like one of those ads on the TV, those public awareness ones. Maybe you could get a job as a voiceover?'

'If you get too sunburnt you'll overheat and so will the baby.'

That shuts her up.

'How you going to cook the mussels?' she asks.

I take a pan out of the bag. 'Steam them, using wet seaweed.'

'Get you, the beach bum chef.'

I tell her it's a trick I learnt at Cadets.

'Didn't know Cadets taught you how to cook, thought they were more about shootin' things, killin' things.'

'I know how to shoot rabbits and skin them, and I know how to catch fish with my hands and gut them. They taught me survival skills and also discipline.'

'I don't think I could kill anything, even if I was hungry.'

'Hunger has no conscience,' I say.

'Where did you read that?'

'I didn't, I don't read books, remember.'

'Oh, promise me you'll read *The White Colt*. I think it'll change your mind about books, you'll so identify with the main character.'

'Because he's a saddo?'

'He's lonely and a misfit but it all changes for him, this chance meeting with this man who has a horse.'

'Does it end happy?'

'Spoiler alert, I didn't actually finish it. Couldn't get past the bit about the hawk.'

'What happens to it?'

'He kills it.'

She takes out a bottle of water from the coolbox and hands it to me.

'He doesn't mean to.'

'That's alright then,' I say.

I lay a small fire. When I'm done I prop an empty packet of cheese and onion crisps on top and then I take out my magnifier.

'Keep your eyes on the first 'o' of onion,' I say.

The sun is on its way down but it's still potent. I target the rays with the magnifier and a small hole appears in the centre of the 'o'.

The hole grows until the 'o' disappears. Keeps on growing until it's taken out the whole word but nothing else happens.

'Is that it?' she says.

'There's supposed to be flames. The rays can't be strong enough.'

'It's OK, you can set alight to something tomorrow when you show me one of your experiments. Don't look like that, you promised you'd show me.'

Martha rings. The food's arrived.

'I'm looking forward to seeing what sort of tests you do. I bet you get all excited like a puppy dog.'

I head off to get the food.

'While you're there you can ask your girlfriend for some matches,' she shouts after me.

Martha opens the door as I walk up the path.

'Saw you coming,' she says. 'Your pop's in that bag and your grub's in this one.'

She holds up two brown paper bags. She's got that permanent sea burnt look people who live by the coast have, when she smiles little white creases appear at the corner of her eyes.

'It came to just short of thirty pounds. I'll add it to your bill.'

I say thanks and take the bags.

'You got free spring rolls an' prawn crackers too, so you won't go hungry. An' I've thrown in a bottle of champagne, free of charge. You can thank those stupid honeymooners who cancelled, they ordered bottles of the stuff, seems only right you and your girl have it.'

She's got the same accent as Tilly, Fee's friend, only Martha's accent isn't fake and neither is she.

'Don't suppose you've got any matches? We thought we'd have a campfire on the beach but we forgot to bring anything to light it with.'

She tells me she won't be a minute. As I wait there's a rap at the window. It's Tom, he wants me to come in. I show him the food but the next thing I know he's at the door and I'm following him into the lounge.

'Got something I want to show you,' he says. He's got the same sea salty look as his wife. 'What do you think of that?'

He points at a half-built model of a tall ship sitting in the middle of a big round table, which is covered in newspaper.

'How long do you think it took me?'

The newspaper is littered with what looks like matchsticks but as I get closer I see they're not matchsticks at all but very short, very thin pieces of balsa wood.

'Go on, guess.'

It's about three-foot long and two-foot high, and the hull and deck are completed.

'Two weeks.'

'Started it yesterday, only got the masts left to do. Been at it all day and all night. Don't sleep much these days. Never was what you'd call a deep sleeper, but these last few years, this bloody heat, nightmare. I said to myself, Tom, you might as well be doing something, so I come downstairs and before I know it, it's morning. Least it stops me disturbing the missus.'

He gives me a knowing wink as Martha appears.

'I don't think our guests want to listen to what you get up to in the middle of the night, Tom.'

She's got a box of Swan Vestas in her hands and drops them into one of the paper bags I'm holding. 'Make sure you stamp it right out when you're done and keep well away from the dunes. We don't want them catching fire, broadcasting what you've been up to. Oh, and tomorrow you're both welcome to join us for something to eat. We usually eat about half six on a Sunday. Got a nice piece of cold ham.'

I thank her and try to leave but Tom hasn't finished.

'Always know how long it takes me from start to finish cos I always use that day's paper when I begin. This one's yesterday's, so you can see I wasn't lying.'

Friday 17th June 2022 is printed at the top of the double spread. There's a headline underneath it.

Tom carries on talking but I'm too busy reading. *DEATH CONFIRMED IN WAREHOUSE FIRE.* That's what it says. They've used block capitals, thick black type. I scan the column below.

Mr Robert Tate. Fifty-four. Walthamstow. They've identified the guard from his dental records.

There's another heading. It's smaller, only two words long.

I read it and the words roll around inside my head. Knock into each other. Keep knocking into each other all the way back to the beach. Hear them with each step.

Watch. Found.

Watch. Found.

Fee snatches the bag from my hands. Moans as she unpacks about how long I took, about the fire not being lit, about the food being cold.

'Matches?' she asks.

I point at one of the bags. When she sees the champagne her mood changes. She hands me the matchbox and I tell her there's no point lighting a fire, it's too warm and I don't want the mussels anymore. I don't want anything.

'I've never sat around a campfire on a beach before, Luke. I want to do that, I want to tick that box. It's already laid. Is this because you have to resort to matches, can't use your spyglass thing?'

I take out a match. I run it along the sandpaper, hear the friction just before the head flares. The smell of sulphur hits my nose as the thin stick bursts into life.

Bet they couldn't believe their luck. *Hey, guv, we found a watch, and guess what? There's a name engraved on the back. It's only his first name but this Luke guy, he was in the Cadets and there's a graduation date engraved there too. How much more do we need? That'll do nicely.*

'Luke!'

The flame has eaten the stick and is about to start on my fingers. I drop the skinny black corpse just in time.

'Are we having a fire or not?'

There's a breeze coming in from the sea. I tell Fee where to sit to block it. It takes a few attempts, but the paper soon lights and then the kindling does too. I build it gradually. Throw on a few twigs at a time. When I'm happy it's taken hold, I snap a bleached branch in half. It makes a loud crack. Cracks even more on the fire. Fee wants to throw something on, asks me to pass her the other half. I tell her to wait.

'You can't throw everything at it, you have to feed it slowly, carefully. Too much and it'll go out.'

'You've caught the sun too,' she says. 'Your face is all red.'

'I am sitting in front of a campfire.'

She grabs a fistful of sand and throws it across the fire at me. Some of it falls into it. The flames hiss like snakes.

'Can I have a look?' Fee asks. 'At your magnifier.'

I take the magnifier out of its pouch, hold it out towards her. 'Don't drop it into the sand, it'll scratch the surface, and don't stand too near the fire with it.'

Fee examines the palm of her left hand with it then turns it on me. Checks my face out with it. 'God, you're even uglier close up.'

I chuck the other half of the branch on the fire. The flames spark and twist their way through it and I think about the night on the Heath. The way the firelight threw shadows, the way Fee fell asleep in my arms. First time I'd spent the night with anyone. Remember how good it felt to not be alone, to have her fill my head and not the dark.

'You could use this as a monocle.'

Fee stands, magnifier to her eye, looking directly at the sun. I lunge at her and punch the glass out of her hand. It spins away and I try and catch it before it falls but I miss.

Fee calls me a fucking moron and I call her a fucking idiot. I pick the magnifier up. It's peppered with sand. I gently blow it away and slip it back inside the pouch.

Fee's sitting on the towels, holding her hand to her chest. 'You've broken my fucking wrist and all you're worried about is your stupid fucking spy glass.'

I kneel beside her and she leans away.

'Don't come near me, stay the fuck away.'

'You could have blinded yourself, Fee.'

I remind her about the crisp packet, what the sun did to it, how it scorched out a neat little hole in seconds.

'That's what could have happened to you,' I say. 'Now show me your hand.'

She relaxes her grip and lets me look. There's a red mark where I caught her, but she's able to twist and bend it.

'I wasn't even looking at the sun.'

I test her pain level by pressing lightly with my fingers. She winces a bit but there's no sign of a break.

'My fault, I should have warned you.'

Fee cradles her wrist as I plate out the food.

'That's twice you've hurt me today,' she whimpers.

I stab at a piece of meat covered in orange gunk. It sticks to the roof of my mouth and I have to swill it down with coke. The food is tasteless, chewy. I throw my fork onto the plate. Throw the plate onto the sand.

'Don't you like it?'

'Not keen on cold food.'

'That's because you took too long to get it. What were you doing? You were in such a foul mood when you came back.'

'You talk such crap.'

'Least I talk. It's like squeezing a fart out of a nit getting anything out of you.'

'Nits don't fart.'

'I know they don't, I'm being ironic.'

I know what's she's being. I want to tell her that reading books and going to a posh school doesn't make you clever, it just makes you lippy.

'I was making conversation. They invited us over to eat with them tomorrow night. I couldn't just take the bags and scarper.'

'What's on the menu?'

I tell her it's cold ham and she doesn't look impressed.

'It's a free meal,' I say.

She gives up trying to eat her food with one hand and takes the champagne out of the carrier bag. She gives it a good shake before she picks at the wire hairnet. Soon as she removes it, it shoots off with an almighty pop.

'It's only champagne,' she says, catching the look on my face.

'It's still alcohol.'

'I am allowed the occasional drink. The medics all agree on that now.'

She fills her glass. The foam bubbles over and she sweeps up the froth with her tongue.

'You know there are laws to stop you drinking and driving,' I say. 'If you're over the limit and you so much as get inside a car, you get prosecuted, but if you're stopped in the street and breathalysed and you're found to be over the limit you're allowed to carry on. Doesn't matter if you're three, four times over it. As long as you don't appear drunk and disorderly, that's OK. You can step out into the road and cause an accident, you can go home and beat up your wife and kids.'

Fee cocks her head to one side, talks to the bucket like it's her friend. 'I think someone needs to tell us something, I think someone had a bit of a drink problem and they don't want to admit it.'

'You're not funny.'

Fee crawls on all fours towards me. I shuffle up to let her sit beside me and she slips her arm through mine.

'Why don't we stay here? The three of us. Me, you, baby. Tom said they were thinking of selling up and going to live in Scotland.'

'That's because they know it won't be safe to live here.'

'You're making it sound like Armageddon's around the corner.'

She lays her head on my lap. 'I'm so tired.'

Fee yawns, rubs her eyes and lies down in front of the fire like a cat. The flames are smaller and they're more restless. I watch them dart and flicker. They're searching, seeking, but there's no more fuel. They'll die soon and so will the fire.

The nearer you get towards your goal, the more at risk you are of not achieving it. I've seen others bottle it, fail to complete the set exercises, fail to reach the finish line. All that work, all that effort, wasted. The setting sun has turned the sky blood red. I'm being sent a warning, but I don't need to be warned. Too much has gone before, too much has been sacrificed.

I have to make two trips, one to take the stuff back and the second to collect Fee. I carry her in my arms and she sleep-slurs all the way back to the lighthouse. The stone steps are narrow, awkward. The only way up is to give her a fireman's lift. She still doesn't wake.

I lie her down on the bed, brush the sand off her face. She pushes my hand away and I leave her be. I make myself an iced coffee and then check the news. One channel is covering food shortages, another desalination plants. Sky's got a heatwave special on how to look after pets and old people. They run a story about the rescue of an old lady. Her neighbour found her on the kitchen floor almost dead from dehydration because she'd been too busy looking after her two dogs and three cats to take care of herself. I think about Mrs Goldman. She'd give her last drop of water to Charlie.

A weekly roundup of fires and deaths follows. It's all looking a lot better, the newscaster says. Definite signs of stability. How much do they love that word.

I select news updates for London and the South East. It's Samia, the young Asian one. The warehouse fire is back at top billing.

'A recent arson attack at a north London warehouse is now being treated as a murder investigation. A body found at the site is now thought to have been deliberately set on fire. A spokesman for London Fire Brigade has described it as one of the most sinister arson attacks he's ever seen. She confirmed a watch had been found at the site but couldn't say whether this was being treated as evidence or not.'

Samia always sounds as if it's her first time at reading the news. Stilted. That's the word.

'It's a significant lead at this stage. The police have described finding the watch as a major breakthrough. They don't wish to release any further details at present, but their investigations are focused on tracing the owner. They have indicated the watch is most likely to have belonged to someone who worked outdoors or took part in outdoor activities. Anyone with any information is encouraged to come forward. At this stage we are seeking to identify and eliminate the owner of the watch. Any contact will be treated in the strictest of confidence.'

She mentions a reward and a number to ring. A red banner appears along the bottom of the screen, it runs on a loop, constantly displaying the number. I have to rewind, watch the coverage again. Need to make sure I don't miss anything.

Sunday, 19th June 2022

My neck isn't too happy with me sleeping on the sofa, nor is my head, and when I open my eyes sunlight stabs its way through to the back of my skull. I turn away and wait for the pain to ease. I left the TV on, can hear the staged squabbling of the morning news teams. My phone rings and I pull the remote out from underneath me and switch the TV off. It's Fee, she's in the cold tub on the upstairs balcony. Wants me to join her. Bring ice cream, she says, then tells me to go commando, because she has.

I fill two bowls with ice cream and take them up. She looks like one of those supermodels, the way she's sitting in the cold tub, hair piled up on her head, her Hollywood shades. I hand her a bowl and climb in. She pushes her sunglasses up on top of her head and screws up her nose.

'Vanilla?'

I say that's all there was, but I didn't actually check. She flips her glasses back down.

'This is a crazy kind of breakfast,' I say.

'I'm a crazy kind of girl.'

She rubs her foot against my leg, playful like.

'I'm in such a good mood this morning. Must be the baby, it must be sending me good vibes.'

Mum was like that with Celine. Celine made Mum happy. I made her sick and I made her put on so much weight her skin stretched so tight it nearly split in two. Mum used to trot that story out a lot.

167

Loved telling everyone that even before I was born, I was giving her grief.

'I want to know about the sugar and the mirrors. I want you to tell me everything and don't go all secretive on me. I like science things. I want to know about your interests, your hobbies. I don't care how kooky they might sound. I'm kooky.'

'What do you want to know?'

'You could start telling me about your tests, why you do them, what you do with all that info. I know you told me something at the Heath but I was in a bad mood, I didn't really take any notice.

'I test the strength of the sun because I think it's dying.'

'That's not news, even I know it's going to die some time.'

'Global warming's being used to scapegoat the fact the sun has already entered its death phase. That's the reason for the change in temperatures. The sun is overheating and it's going die pretty soon.'

'So, it's not global warming?'

'Correct.'

'But why would it do that?'

'Because we've forsaken it. Early cultures used to pay their respects, show their reverence. They knew how central the sun was to life and they paid homage it. They had festivals, carried out rituals, made offerings. We don't do that anymore. We've taken it for granted, and we're being punished.'

I wait for the disbelief to show in her eyes, wait for her to turn away, try and hide her smile.

'Do you carry out rituals?'

'I do, I make offerings, leave tributes. Fruit, roadkill.'

'OMG, did you offer up the dead squirrel? You did, didn't you? Did it help? Was the sun pleased?'

I don't know if she's taking the piss now and I wish I hadn't said anything.

'Needs more than a bite-sized snack to please the sun now,' I say.

'Why, how long have we got before it dies? I mean we talking hundreds of years, thousands of years, hundreds of thousands of years?'

'Three days,' I say.

Now she doesn't know whether *I'm* taking the piss or not.

I crack a smile and she flicks ice cream at me. I do the same back, flick it all over her face.

'Lick if off then,' she says. 'If we only got three days left we better make the most of it.'

I lick her cheeks, her nose, her lips. Fee wants to climb on top of me. I ask if she's sure, that I don't want to hurt the baby. You won't, she says, grinding her hips into mine. We have sex and then we have more sex, and the last time is better than the time before, and then Fee gets out of the tub and lies on the decking. I feel the sun on my back as we fuck. The tattoo burning into me. I'm either being marked, branded, or the sun is giving me its blessing.

'Whoa, easy tiger,' Fee murmurs. 'You're pushing too hard, slow down.'

'Nearly there,' I say.

'Luke.' She pushes my shoulders away. 'Slow down.' Tries to wriggle free. 'Stop. Please, stop.'

'Soon,' I say.

'I said stop. Luke! Luke!'

She screams and I stop. I roll away, lie on the deck tensing, twitching. I can't stop it. I can't stop the pleasure running through me, I just have to let it be.

'When I say stop, I mean stop,' Fee says, her voice breaking. 'I don't mean carry on. For someone who didn't want to have sex in case they hurt the baby you sure didn't seem to mind hurting me.'

I tell her I got carried away, that it won't happen again.

'No, it won't. You're dead right about that.'

She leaves me on the decking, goes back inside. The cold tub bubbles away like a kettle on the boil. I switch it off and follow her. Her damp footprints evaporate so quickly by the time I step inside they've completely gone.

The bedroom door is shut. I rap on it, but Fee doesn't answer. I tell her I'm going to take a shower. She still doesn't reply.

I let the water drill into me, turn the power up to max. Want to flush away the thought that maybe I couldn't stop because it wouldn't let me. I felt like that with Mum. Like it had me in its grip. And just now it did not want to let me go.

After I've showered, I check on Fee again. This time the bedroom door is ajar. I stand outside, fiddle with the towel wrapped around my hips, then push it open.

'Is this a Dad thing, or is this a me thing, or is this a baby thing? Because there is a thing. You are not the Luke I know, I don't recognise you.'

She's on the bed in one of her big sloppy t-shirts. I walk towards

169

her and she puts out her hands.

'Don't come any nearer.'

I ask if I can sit on the end of the bed and she says OK. I sit down and rest my hands on my knees. They look broader, bigger-knuckled, like his hands.

'I swear it won't happen again.'

'Swear on your life.'

'OK. I swear on my life.'

'Swear on the baby's life.'

'There is no baby to swear on yet.'

'It won't always be this small. In a few months it'll be humongous. Why do you have to be so tall? I'm a bit scared this baby's going to rip my insides out.'

It would scare me, pushing a thing the size of a football out of my body.

'Kangaroos have got it sorted. They crawl into their mother's pockets when they're the size of a maggot, stay there until it's time to hop out.'

'It's not just giving birth I'm scared of, Luke. I don't know how we're going to manage. We've only just met and now we're going to be a ready-made family? What we going do about money, where we going to live? I'm really worried, to be honest. You must be too.'

'It'll be OK.'

'How, you work in a garage and I'm still at school.'

She sighs and I get up, reach underneath the bed. I pull the rucksack out, hit her on the chin with the first bundle. The second hits her shoulder. I keep throwing them, one after the other. Money piles up around her and all she can do is stare.

'Five hundred in each,' I say.

She picks one up.

'I got a promotion. That's my back pay, plus an advance.'

She rips the bundle open and chucks it in the air. Picks up another and does the same.

She's like a kid in a sweet shop. Feels good to make her feel this way. Feels good to be able to do something right.

Sometimes you know you're dreaming. You know what's happening isn't actually happening and you know all you have to do is sit tight and wait. It's like watching a movie because that's what it is, it's a movie running inside your head. A movie that plays out in front of you that you've written and star in, but don't know the plot. The twists and turns, they're all a surprise, as is the ending. Sometimes it's fun, sometimes it's so entertaining you wish you could do it all the time. But when it's not that kind of movie, when it's a big bad scary type. When it's a horror movie that you really don't want to watch but you have to because sleep has you prisoner. That's not fun, that's fucking torture.

I'm at the edge of a volcano, looking down into a crater of boiling magma. Pockets of gas bubble up through the nuclear gloop and the air stinks from the sulphur. Mum's with me and I'm happy because she isn't dead, she didn't die. She's right there, breathing and smiling, and then she walks forward, steps off the edge and I can't stop her. I close my eyes, too scared to look, wait for the scream but it doesn't come because she hasn't fallen. She's hanging in the air, suspended above the hot mass, arms spread wide like an angel. I scream at her, plead with her to come back but she won't. She tips backwards until she's horizontal, flat on her back, hovering a few feet above the furnace. And I still hope. I still hope she'll be OK, and then she drops.

I have no choice but to watch, witness the heat melt her skin, her hair. Witness her buck and twist like cardboard on a bonfire, like the guard would have done at the warehouse. I am forced to watch her body bend and curve. All I can do is scream. Keep on screaming until the movie's over.

The nightmare ends and I wake but the screaming continues. Because it's not me doing the screaming, it's Fee. She's hiding under the duvet. The room is in total darkness and thunder is rolling around above us like a giant steel ball. I check the time, it's only four in the afternoon. The last thing I remember is the pair of us, rolling around in the money, getting so high, eating each other alive. The thunder builds and then it crashes into the room and I'm up out of bed, running to the window. There's a corker of a storm going on outside. The sky thick as smoke, every bit of blue choked from it. In the distance flashes of lightning rip down to the sea and there's nothing calm or flat about the sea anymore. It heaves, churns. Filthy as the sky.

I tell Fee to come out and watch and she tells me to fuck off. Another roll of thunder shakes the window. The storm's coming in across the sea and it's heading towards us at such a pace. I watch the lightning speed in at us, watch the streaks branch, split into forks. When it hits the sea there's a flash of power so violent it seems to light up the whole sky.

'I hate thunderstorms,' Fee says.

I turn around, tell her to stay put, it will soon be over, but when I turn to look back a bolt as thick as a tree trunk flexes and arcs right outside the window. It writhes around like a living thing, fills the room with so much brilliance, a hundred, a thousand times brighter than any stadium. It's Frankenstein. Pure fucking Frankenstein.

The storm moves inland, leaves behind the kind of rain we normally get in the wet season. Vertical, never ending. Fee doesn't want to go out in it. I remind her we haven't any food in and that a takeway delivery won't be very likely.

'The storm will have blown over by then, we got hours yet. Even if it hasn't the cottage is only down the causeway. It'll have eased off by then.

The storm stays put all day and so do we. Fee wants to watch movies and I want to go watch it from the viewing platform but she doesn't want to be on her own, so we watch a movie. A budget zombie romance.

I like how comfortable it feels. The two of us on the sofa, Fee resting her legs on my lap.

'There'll be a baby in a few months and then the three of us will be all cuddled up on the sofa,' Fee says.

'Thanks,' I say and kiss the top of her head.

'What for?'

'Giving me everything I ever wanted.'

'You're welcome. Quick, the ending's coming up, it's the best bit,' Fee says.

The zombie bride and groom are at the altar exchanging their vows. As they lean in for the kiss the screen goes black. I say it must be down to the storm and Fee fills me in about the ending. I pretend to be interested and the screen comes back to life but it's showing an alert, not the film.

SOLAR ALERT FORECAST TOMORROW
CHECK LOCAL NEWS FOR DETAILS
STAY SUN SAFE

'How can there be a solar alert?' Fee says. 'It's fucking raining, there is no sun.'

A weather map of northern Europe flashes up. The eye of the storm is situated at the top of Spain. We've just had the first wave of it. A line tracks its movements over the next twenty-four hours. It'll brush the southwest coast of England, and the west coast of Wales, but Ireland's going to take a direct hit.

I press the green button for more info. *The hurricane will continue to lessen in severity as it skirts the southwest coast of the UK but warnings will be in operation tonight and into the early hours of tomorrow morning. Ireland could see unprecedented storm levels and risk to life warnings are in place across Ireland and parts of Wales. Anyone wishing to travel in the UK should refer to regional updates. Following the storm, a band of unusually high pressure could push temperatures to fifty degrees.*

'Fifty degrees. Blimey. Fortune went to Spain last year, said it was over fifty in the south. I guess you get used to it. Actually, it'll be nice to have a bit of a heatwave after all this rain.'

'Haven't you listened to anything? All you can talk about is a fucking heatwave? This isn't a heatwave.'

The film comes back on and the zombie couple, dressed in wedding gear, are eating each other. They keep doing it until all that's left is their heads. Their heads roll around in the church, bang into the pews, as they try and to take bites out of each other's faces.

'That was crap,' I say.

'Not a fan of zombie movies, then? Why didn't you say, we could have watched updates about the weather.'

'This isn't just a bad day at the beach. This is serious. Why do you think we've got freak weather systems happening all over the world? It's not just happening here in little old UK. California's a dustbowl. Africa's a desert. The sun is going into meltdown, right in front of us, and all you can do is mock. You'll still want me to save you though, won't you? You and all the other Ungratefuls.'

'Ungratefuls?'

'We should get ready soon, they're expecting us.'

'I'm not going anywhere in this weather.'

I remind her we've no food in, and the odds on having a takeaway delivered in the middle of a storm aren't good. Fee looks at the windows. The driving rain makes it impossible to see out.

'Most people, most rational people, believe the sun has got at least another trillion, billion years to go.'

'That's a good estimate for a mathematician,' I say. 'If you'd been listening properly, you'd know that's not true.'

'I think the sun's fried your brain, maybe you should stay out of it forever.'

It wasn't a volcano. It was the sun. It was the sun that had Mum in its grip. It was a warning. The time is coming and I need to be ready.

The cottage is less than fifty yards away but when we reach it it's as if we've fallen off the causeway into the sea and climbed back out of it. We both hammer on the door and it's Tom lets us in.

'Here, dry yourselves with these,' he says, handing us a towel each. 'We get some rum weather these days, don't we? They're like a pair of drowned rats!' he shouts down the hall. 'There's sou'westers at the lighthouse and wellies. Didn't you see them? Never mind, we got spares, and a canoe if you need it.'

Martha pops her head around the kitchen door. 'He's only winding you up. Tom, pour them a drink and keep them entertained. Dinner won't be long, my lovelies.'

'Go on, in you go.' Tom hurries us into the lounge.

The smell of gravy coming from the kitchen wakes my stomach up. I turn around to apologise for the noise it makes and catch Tom ogling Fee's arse. We walk into the front room and I see the ship he was working on has gone and so too the newspapers. The dining table is now covered with a white tablecloth and laid out with silvery cutlery and in the middle is a large bottle of champagne.

'You wonderin' what happened to the Bounty?' Tom asks. 'I finished it this mornin'. It's upstairs in the attic now with the others. Shall have to start another soon.'

Me and Fee stand in front of the open fire. It's a farmhouse one with a big black grate and a big brass bucket for logs and a big wooden mantelpiece. I can see there's four empty glasses on the mantle. Tom walks over to us with the champagne bottle off the table. He opens it like a pro and pours us each a drink. When he hands Fee her glass his tongue does this weird thing. Darts in and out like he's after a taste of her and I wish her t-shirt hadn't got as wet and clingy.

He offers me a drink and I tell him no thanks but he either doesn't hear me or he wasn't listening, so I take it. The storm's tailing off but there's still the odd rumble. Softer, quieter now.

'Reckon Ireland are going to get it bad. Got the army on standby, much good it'll do 'em if the predictions are correct,' Tom says.

'Luke's Irish,' Fee says.

'No I'm not,' I say.

'Oh, sorry, thought you were. My mistake.'

Tom winks at Fee. 'Must have been the boyfriend before,' he says. 'Isn't your surname Irish?'

'No.'

Tom pats the sofa. It's one of those shiny brown leather types that look as comfy as a mattress but when you sit on them they're like sitting on fucking concrete. 'Come on, sit yourselves down. You two have the Chesterfield and I'll have me old armchair. Too straight backed that thing. Bit too stiff for me.'

'Spargo doesn't sound at all Irish,' I say to Fee.

'It would if you put an 'O' in front, as well as at the end,' Tom quips.

Fee says O'Spargo a few times, then takes a drink. It goes down the wrong way.

'You OK, love? Not used to drinking, is that it? Sorry, I was forgetting myself. Should've asked first.'

'No, it's fine. I like a drink.'

'My kind of woman.' Tom winks at her and I can see he's having trouble keeping that lizard tongue of his still. I give him a look. He takes this as me wanting to ask something and the chin juts out and the head tilts back, to let me know he's ready.

'So, you two been together long?'

''Bout a year.'

I go to correct her and she presses her hand into my arm to stop me.

'Must be serious. And how old are you both, if you don't mind me asking?'

'Luke's twenty-one and I'm eighteen.'

I drum my fingers on the stem of the glass.

'Really?'

'How old did you think we were?'

'Now you're asking, you could be thirteen, you could be thirty. Everyone under fifty looks the same to me. Too bloody young!'

He sits back in his chair. 'I was married at twenty-one, three kids by twenty-six. Live your life first, that's what I say, before you start going having a family, settling down. Enjoy your youth while you can.'

'We intend to,' Fee looks at me with an over-the-top loved-up face and I wish she'd stop with the play-acting.

'You planning on getting wed then, is that why you came here – check it out first? Very romantic place, this, you know. We get lots of honeymooners.'

'I'll go and see if Martha needs any help,' I say, putting my drink down on the side table.

'Don't you dare, you sit right back down. My wife will bring it out when she's good and ready. Women don't like to be rushed. That's something I've learnt over the years.'

He winks at me and parts his lips. I catch sight of the tip of his tongue and I wish we hadn't come. The storm has died right down and we might have been able to order a pizza after all. Fee finishes her champagne and holds her glass out for more. I swap her empty one with my full one.

'So, what do you do then? As a job.'

Tom's asking me but Fee's there again.

'Luke's studying to be a lawyer.'

'Oh, brainy and good-looking, got yourself a good catch there, girl. So where do you do this studying then?'

'Cambridge.'

Easy as squeezing toothpaste.

'Now, I think that calls for another drink!' He leans forward to pick up the bottle and I see him wince, like he's pulled a muscle. 'Shouldn't really have too much of the good stuff. Least that's what the doctors say. But what do they know, eh? Come on, Luke, you've got an empty glass there.'

I tell him I don't drink and he turns to Fee. 'All the better for us then. Spargo, eh? That's a Cornish name if I'm not mistaken, your family from the south west?'

I shake my head.

'Only, I knew a Spargo from when I lived in Boscastle. Funny bloke. Wasn't your Dad, was it?'

'His Dad's from up north,' Fee says.

I glare at her but she's too busy looking at Tom. I don't like that she's letting him know my name, where I'm from.

Martha appears at the door, two full plates in her hand. She asks Tom to go and get the gravy.

As he pushes himself up from his chair he steadies himself and I see him wince again.

'Now then, you two, sit yourselves down at the table and tuck in.

Don't wait for us.' She lays a roast dinner down in front of us and follows Tom into the kitchen and we sit down next to each other at the table.

I pick up my knife and fork and Fee frowns at me. 'She said we could start.'

'It's polite to wait,' she says.

'Is it polite to go telling so many lies?'

'It's a bit of fun. I haven't had that much fun lately, and at least I'm making an effort, you've hardly opened your mouth.'

'Is the dinner OK?' Tom's back with the gravy and Fee gives him a thumbs up even though she hasn't eaten any. He sets the gravy boat down on the table and Martha arrives with two more plates. When they sit down Tom insists on a toast.

'To Fee and Luke, may your life be filled with as much love and laughter as ours has been.'

Everyone says hear, hear and I nod, can't speak because I've got a mouthful of food.

Tom drools all the way through dinner and it's not over the cooking. Fee loves the attention and the banter. I can't join in because I'm not relaxed enough to think of anything funny or witty, I'm too busy staring at the centre of the table, where the newspaper was. Keep seeing those two words. That's all that's in my head.

Watch Found. Watch Found.

Tom's tongue is out again. I wonder if I'm the only one to notice.

'Your stomach giving you gip again, Tom?' his wife says. She pours him a glass of water. 'It's the Yorkshire puds. Tom loves 'em but they give 'im terrible indigestion. Either that or I've poisoned him!'

Fee finds this hilarious. 'I thought Luke was going to poison us,' she hiccoughs. 'I told him you couldn't pick mussels in July, said there's got to be an 'r' in the month. But it's the other way around! I got it completely wrong.'

I try and explain we didn't actually eat them anyway but no one's listening.

'Not to worry, we get guests eating them whether there's an 'r' in the month or not.' Martha tops her glass up with the rest of the champagne. 'I mean, what's the worst it can do?'

'Kill you!' Fee shrieks.

It sets the others off. The three of them roll around laughing and it feels like they're laughing at me.

'Isn't this grand? We're like one big happy family,' Martha says.

'We didn't actually eat them,' I explain again, as they clink glasses together.

'Cheers all,' Fee says. Not even hearing me or realising I haven't joined in. She's not alone, none of them have noticed.

It was the same at home. All I ever wanted to do was finish eating and fuck off. It was a punishment being made to sit at the table. Mum twisting herself up trying to sidestep Dad's landmines, defuse the ticking bomb before your dinner would end up sliding down the wall.

I try and pour Fee a glass of water but she doesn't want it, sticks her hand over her glass and gets it wet. She tells me off and I pass her my napkin to dry her hand with and then I make an excuse about needing the loo.

'There's one under the stairs, love,' Martha says.

Tom's inspecting the bruise on Fee's wrist when I come back. The one she got when I punched the magnifier away.

'Anyway, I nearly got blinded but Luke saved me.'

Fee pulls her hand away as I sit down and then that gap in the conversation, the one that naturally opens up in readiness for the explanation. The explanation to put everyone at ease and allow the chit chat to start up again. They're waiting for me to say how the smudge of a bruise got there. Because that's all it is, a smudge, nowhere near the size of the bruise on Fee's leg. Everyone's staring at me. All I need to do is say what happened, tell them the truth. That I was trying to stop her from getting blinded. But I just sit there in silence.

Fee tells them what happened, and Tom looks at me in a way that makes me think he doesn't believe her. In a way that says he thinks I've told her to say that.

'Well, that was a stupid thing to do, wasn't it! Who's a silly girl, eh? Promise Tom you won't do it again.'

He pinches Fee hard on the cheek, grabs a big chunk of it like you would a kid, and I can tell she's as embarrassed as I am. Want to tell Martha she needs to reel him in, keep him under control, stick a muzzle on him.

'Learnt your lesson there, missy,' is all she says.

I wonder if this is normal. Wonder if he does it so much she's got used to it, doesn't notice anymore, or that it's best to ignore him.

'That could have been nasty,' Tom says, looking at me. 'The sun's a strong and powerful thing. I was only reading about it the other day. There was this article—'

'The ham's delicious,' I say, to Martha.

'Well, there's plenty more, so help yourself. Heard you Londoners 'aven't 'ad fresh meat for weeks. We're lucky, our local farmer makes sure we get what we need before they send it off to market. But they'll have to declare everything, once the government inspectors get here. Heaven knows when it's all going to stop. The poor cattle, though. I do feel sorry for 'em in this heat.'

She leans across and forks a slice of meat onto her plate. 'Sorry, love, what were you going to say?'

I try and butt in but Tom's up on his feet, clearing his throat.

'The pollution up there' – he sticks a finger up at the ceiling – 'traps the heat down here.' He raps his knuckles on the table. 'Reflects it back, the way a strip of foil behind a radiator does.'

The slow talking, the little touch of drama, he's got all the skills of a crap teacher.

'Only the pollution's not only keeping the heat in, it's keeping the light out, so that means we're getting more heat and less sunlight. Global dimming, they call it, it's linked to global warming.'

'Bullshit,' I say.

'Which, global dimming or global warming?'

'Both.'

'Oh no, no, no, no.' Tom's finger goes into overdrive. 'It most certainly is not bullshit. All the facts confirm it. The data's been verified by scientists and experts from every corner of the globe, you can't argue with facts, lad.'

'What about independent researchers? Those free of government funding and government control, what if their facts showed something different?'

'Oh, I got you now. You're one of those Unbelievers, one of those armchair amateurs.' Tom clasps his hands around his fat gut, which has grown fatter from all the food and booze he's stuffed inside it.

'Unbelievers. Now are they the ones that think it's not happening, or are they the ones that think it is? I can't keep up with it.' Martha shakes her head and looks at Fee.

'Believers are the ones that believe in global warming because they are the ones that listen to reason, listen to facts. Unbelievers are the ones that don't believe, they think it's all a big conspiracy,' Tom explains. 'Am I right, young sir?'

He holds his hand out to me, as if he's giving me permission to speak.

'I'm neither. They're both wrong.'

He doesn't know what to say now. Thought he had me pegged.

'Luke reckons the sun is dying, that's why it's getting hotter, because it's going into meltdown. That's right, isn't it, Luke?'

They way she's talking about it, all casual. They way she's thrown it in, as if it's just an aside.

'Shut up,' I whisper.

'He can prove it, he's got records and everything. Does experiments with mirrors and things.'

I kick her leg under the table. She pretends not to notice.

Tom folds his arms, puts on a patronising voice, to go with his patronising face. 'There are very learned people, scientists who spend years, lifetimes, studying their speciality. Their work gets tested and re-tested. You can't do your own tests. You can't come up with your own theories and think they're more valid. You'd be a crackpot if you thought that.'

I've gone from *lad* to *sir* to *crackpot*.

'The sun's got billions of years left, lad. Why, it's only just hit middle age, got plenty of life left in it.'

The way he smiles at Fee and the way she smiles back, I have to say it. I tell him to fuck off and Fee gets all cheerleader.

'Go, Luke. Go, Luke.'

Fee bangs the table with her fists and then Martha taps her knife onto her plate. 'Eton Mess, lemon cheesecake, or both!' Martha shouts as she taps.

Fee and Tom chant back both, and just as I'm thinking I can't deal with the noise or the madness, Tom surprises me so much, I almost shake his hand.

'Actually, I don't know if I believe what they say either.'

I don't know if he's messing or if he means it. If anyone's an armchair amateur it's him. All he's done so far is spout stuff he's heard on the TV or read in the newspapers.

'You're right to doubt,' I say. 'It's all lies. They know what's really happening but they're too afraid to go public with it. They'd rather we—'

Tom doesn't want to hear what I've got to say, cuts me off and gives out about how extremes in weather have always existed. Sits there regurgitating the same old rubbish. I should have known.

'Did you know the River Thames iced over in medieval times?' he says. Fee goes all fake-surprised and then he's off lecturing us on glaciers. 'Huge ice masses once travelled all the way from Scotland, cut right through the centre of England. You see, there has always been extremes and there will always be. This freak weather will disappear as quick as it arrived, mark my words.'

He really is the worst kind of wanker. The kind that would fill his pants if he knew what freak weather was really coming. The kind that would sink to his knees, beg me for help, beg me to do something, anything, to save his pathetic little life. But right now he doesn't think I'm worthy of air time. He doesn't think I'm worthy, full stop. They warned us not to expect any thanks, told us that at graduation. Said if anyone was thinking of using their training to go on and serve the country, do not under any circumstances expect gratitude. No one is going to give a bucking bronco that you might want to put your life on the line for theirs. It's a job, that's all, and some poor bastard's got to do it.

'I know how to stop it,' I say.

'OK, let's say for argument's sake, that your hypothesis has a tiny, tiny bit of truth in it. Let's say it could happen, let's stick our necks out and say it is happening. They've already got things to reflect the sun's rays, neutralise emissions so there's no real danger.'

'Ignorance is danger,' I say.

Fee plants her hands on the table, pushes herself up to standing.

'Tom, for your information Luke is a scientist. He studied it at Cambridge and he has a calling, a destiny.'

I take hold of her arm and try and yank her back into her seat, but she won't have it. 'He's got very special powers and he's going to use them to save the world.'

She sticks her arm out in front of her and hums the *Superman* theme, then Tom and Martha join in.

I put my head in my hands and Fee fires a sniper shot at me.

'However, as we all know, experiments need to be carried out in a controlled environment to allow the gathering of reliable evidence. I've seen Superman's calculations and I think there are way too many variables, and the environments are way too uncontrolled, so therefore I declare the results are invalid.'

Fee gets a round of applause because they take what she says at face value. Even though she's not speaking the truth. Sure, she's seen my calculations but she hasn't actually studied them, verified them. All she knows about are the uncontrolled environments but they're not the only environments I use. She doesn't have all the facts, but that doesn't seem to matter. It never does. That's why people never get the truth, because they don't look for it, they accept what they get told, because it's easier.

'I do have a controlled environment.' I say. 'I've got a shed.'

As soon as I say it I wish I hadn't but there's nothing I can do. There's no time lapse feature in the real world, you can't edit what you say, delete the thing you wish you hadn't said. Once it's out, it's out.

'Call off the guards, Superman's got a shed, he's got a shed. We're all going to be fine, we're all going to be saved because he's got a—'

Martha and Fee shout 'shed' at the same time. I look at the three of them enjoying the joke. What hurts most is that I dared to tell her. I dared to share the one thing that mattered with the one person that mattered. Course it had to turn out this way. Course it, I, had to become a joke. Why would I think anything else?

I excuse myself and go to the loo again. It's even smaller than the one at the garage but it's clean and there's bog roll. I sit down on the pan and see this year's calendar is hanging on the back of the door. It's one of those vintage ones. Nostalgic pictures of seaside favourites. June is Torquay and there's a cartoon family on a cartoon beach, having cartoon fun.

I wish the calendar wasn't hanging there, wish I didn't have to look at how close it was. But I do. The date looks as innocent as all the others. June 21st isn't ringed, it's not signposted as anything special, but there is a mark there just above the date. It's only small but it's definitely there, and it's been made by hand, it's been done with a pen. I recognise it. It's one I've seen before. One I've used myself.

Tom meets me in the hall, tells me Fee's been sick and Martha is dealing with, so best we go into the kitchen, he says.

'You must find it very different from London down 'ere. Can't imagine being amongst all those people in all that heat,' Tom says, opening the fridge door. 'Course, it can be too quiet for some folks. Now where she's put the milk?'

I close in, slam the fridge door shut from behind him, push Tom up against it.

'Do you always flirt with schoolgirls? Or you doing that to get her to relax, get her to let down her guard?' I lean against him with all my weight. 'I recognise the sign. The one you got marked on the calendar. What things you got planned for Tuesday? Do they involve us?'

He doesn't look as cocksure with his face squashed up against the door. 'I got a delivery coming Tuesday. A ship, another model ship that's what that is. Martha must have written on it. That's all that is, it's nothing else!'

'Dodgy-looking spot you got there,' I say. 'That one near your eye. Seen pics like that in the leaflets they give out. You should get it looked at. That sun can be deadly.'

'I can't breathe… Please, you're choking me.'

He screws his eyes up as if he's in pain. I see the colour drain from his face. I let go. And he slides to the floor. Looks like a puppet with its strings cut.

Fee battles with the umbrella Martha lent her as we walk back to the lighthouse. It's useless in this wind and it isn't even raining that much.

'You're sleeping on the sofa, I want the bed to myself tonight,' Fee says, dumping the brolly down, upended and still open. I pick it up and close it and leave it at the foot of the stairs. 'What did you do to him?'

'I didn't do anything. He fainted, that's all.'

'You can't kick off every time someone flirts me with me. I can take care of myself.'

My phone buzzes in my pocket, it's on silent so I let it vibrate.

'You didn't have to do it.'

'Do what?' I say, looking to see if the caller leaves a message.

'Kill her.'

I look up at her, try and remember where I was when I dreamt of Mum, whether it was the night Fee heard me call out, or if it was another night or another nightmare.

'The wasp,' she says. 'The hornet, you didn't have to kill it. You didn't have to do what I asked you to. You've been in a bad mood ever since.'

She storms off up the stairs and I listen to Malik's message. It's garbled but I get the gist. The police have rumbled Kojak's scam and he's been arrested, along with Irish. Walked into the garage yesterday morning, cuffed him. Closed the place down.

Sounds like Scarlet's with him and he must get distracted, moves the phone away from his mouth. I can't hear him but then he's back loud and clear. They want to speak to you too, he says. Something about a warehouse you and Kojak visited. They asked if you gone away, seem to think you got on a train at Paddington.

I'm breathing so fast it's making me dizzy. I can't listen anymore.

Fee won't let it rest about Tom. Wants to ring, see how he is, says we should haven't left when we did. She tells me again I'm sleeping on the sofa.

'We're not sleeping anywhere,' I say. 'We need to pack, we need to go. That storm was just a taster, there's another one coming. Curfews will be in place from dawn. If we leave now we can get back to London in time.'

'Now, you want to go now?'

'You can stay if you want, but I'm heading back.'

Fee's bag thumps down the lighthouse steps, one at a time.

'Hurry up, the cab won't wait forever,' I shout up to her.

She drags her bag off the last step, points at the red and yellow buckets by the door, full of the mussels we didn't eat.

'They still alive?'

'What?'

'We need to put them back. You gave me grief over that one little wasp but you're happy for all those mussels to die?'

I pick her bag up and walk towards the car. A soft drizzle falls on me as I hand the cab driver both bags. He puts them in the boot and I get in.

'Could I ask a favour?' Fee says to the driver. 'Could you take the coast road and wait at the top for five minutes, would you mind doing that? I'm studying marine biology and I need to return these back to their natural environment.'

Fee holds up the buckets for him to see. It's such a see-through lie but he plays along.

'Long as you don't spill anything. Cleaned the car today, waste of time that was.'

'We'll make sure not to spill a drop, won't we, Luke?'

She hands me the buckets and gets in. I manage to get in without any water or mussels being spilt. As the car pulls away the headlights turn the rain into a needle shower. I wish I could take one, pop the doubt, the fear growing inside me. This was not supposed to happen like this. It was not supposed to be such a mess.

We pull up underneath a streetlight.

'Bye, mussels,' Fee says, as the driver opens the passenger door for me.

I look out. The fluorescent lighting only reaches to the grass verge.

'Do you want me to go?' Fee asks.

The driver bends down, speaks to me. 'What, scared of a bit of wind and rain, big boy like you?'

I climb out and tower over him. I'm nearly a foot taller.

'Stay this side of the warning signs,' he says.

I cross the road and step onto the grassed area. The signs are staked into the grassed area that leads to the cliff edge. I've left the safety of the streetlight and I wish I'd brought a torch. I stare into the dark, think about the sun, think about it not being gone, just in another sky. I wonder if it's a gentler one, a less punishing one. Wonder if I've done enough. Whether when it rises tomorrow all will be forgiven.

It's much windier here. The buckets swing wild in my hands and the rain flits around my face and it's even harder to see where I'm going. The warning signs say to go no further, but I can't see the edge so I carry on.

The driver toots and I look back and see the car all lit up, Fee inside it. He toots again and leans out his window, gestures for me to stop. The edge can't be too far away, I can hear the sea hitting the rocks below, can smell the brine. I hurl the red, then the yellow bucket. The wind whips them upwards, then downwards and then the nothingness takes them. They're there and then they're not. Like the light is on and then it's off. Like the sun is here and then it's gone.

'Didn't you hear me shouting you? They're pulling the trains. If we don't leave now, you might not catch the last one out.'

The driver's standing behind me. He tells me to stop messing about and when I don't move, he puts his hand on my shoulder.

It's the tiniest of movements. The smallest of tremors. One you wouldn't even notice during the day. You'd put it down to the strong wind catching you off guard, blowing you a little off balance. It only lasts a second and then it's gone. The thunder lasts longer. It's loud, deafening, but it's not coming from above, it's coming from below. There's been another fall, the cliff face has given way and now the edge is in view because it's come closer.

A second tremor hits. We grab hold of each other, try and stay upright, as the ground beneath us does its best to bring us down. The driver clings on to me and I see the edge is now only a few inches from our feet. He's shaking more than the ground is, and he's in danger of falling forward and taking me with him. If someone has to fall, it can't be me. That cannot happen.

I jab my elbow into his chest, hard as I can. It winds him and I'm able to move away from him. We both stand there knowing the end of the cliff is less than a footstep away. I'm taller and that makes me less stable but he's the one panicking. He reaches his hand out and I swing back my arm and strike him. I catch his jaw and knock him off balance. He whirls his arms around to right himself but then he looks down and that's all it takes. His own body weight goes against him and he pitches forward.

I see it, the realisation in his eyes, the knowledge that this is it, that this will be his final moment. His white shirt balloons out as he falls. I watch it get smaller and smaller as he falls further and further. All I can think of is I'm glad Mum wasn't aware, I'm glad she didn't know.

The keys are still in the ignition. I jump into the driver's seat and start the engine.

'Where's the driver?' Fee asks.

'Give me your phone?'

'What's happened?'

'I need to ring an ambulance, give me your bloody phone. Mine's out of charge.'

I tell her the driver's had a fall, injured himself. Soon as she passes her phone, I throw it out the car. I slam the door and drive away. Fee shouts at me. Wants her phone back. Wants me to stop. Tells me we can't leave the driver, can't just take his car.

'We have to go. There's been landslides along the coast, they've stopped trains running to London. We need to get back to London.'

'Where is he? Where did he fall?' She tries her door, bangs on the window.

I slap the steering wheel, shout at her to calm down. 'He doesn't matter, none of this does. What matters is that we get back in time.'

'For what?'

'For the day of judgement. The day I've been talking about.'

I pick up speed. The roads are twisty and the rain is coming down heavy again. The wipers flick back and forth, smooth, soundless. The visibility isn't good but I need to get as much ground covered as I can, before it becomes a full-on downpour.

I check Fee in the driver's mirror, she's got her head in her hands, but she's quietened down. I look back at the road. There's no other traffic, but the lighting is bad and I don't see the dip in the road. The car glides to the left, keeps gliding left, the wheels have no grip at all.

We aquaplane over to the opposite side of the road, like we're a couple of freewheeling schoolkids on bikes going downhill. I shout at Fee, tell her to sit as close to the nearside door as possible. Tell her to grab hold of the door handle. We bump into the kerb and mount the pavement and Fee swears as she gets thrown around on the back seat. There's no oncoming traffic but there's a lone bus shelter not far ahead. The kerb has slowed the car down enough and the tyres can grip now we're off the road, I'm able to pull on the handbrake before we hit the shelter.

We skid to a halt. I get out the car, open the rear door. The rain is coming down hard, drumming on the roof of the car, beating into my face and chest.

'I'm just trying to do the right thing, that's all. I need to get you and the baby to safety. Tomorrow is just the beginning, Fee. All those disaster movies you've watched, all the YouTube videos you've seen with people frying eggs on the pavement, seeing ice cubes melt in minutes, that's nothing. You think it's going to be a little bit hot for a while, you've no idea. Imagine opening an oven door, feeling that heat hit your face, imagine that on repeat. Imagine that never ever going away. I'm the only one who can stop this. That's why I took the car. I need to get you and the baby to safety. I'm the only one who can stop this because I'm the only one who knows how to stop this. And it was you that wanted me to return the mussels.'

'Stop talking your shit, stop talking like a crazy!'

'"Oh, I'm a marine biologist, could you pull up on the coast road", I say, mocking her voice. 'The driver would still be here if you hadn't had such a crazy idea. You need to take some responsibility and stop making out I'm the one with the problem. It could have been me over that cliff. I could have died too.'

'Died? Is he dead? I thought you said he was injured!'

I get back into the driver's seat and activate the door locks. Fee wrestles with the handle of her door. Keeps on pulling at it. I start the engine.

'You can't take me against my will. Let me out. Please, Luke, just leave me here. I won't say anything, just let me out!'

'There's always casualties, that's what happens in conflict.'

I move off and she kicks the back of my seat. When I won't stop she takes off her seatbelt, leans forward and puts her hands either side of my headrest. Claws at anything she can. I put my foot down on the accelerator. It's a brand new solar hybrid. Nice acceleration, no wonder he didn't want any dirty seawater being spilt. Fee falls backwards, back into her seat. I take a corner at speed and she gets flung around, begs me to slow down. I tell her to put her seatbelt back on and switch on the radio. Fee complies and I slow down to a decent cruise. The car's a good handler and it's got some kick, a near-full tank and it's charged up nicely.

There's a traffic update. The south east isn't too affected. No road closures or train cancellations. The south west and Wales will be hit worst, but the M4 is open and no traffic incidents reported.

As I thought, we won't be in the danger zone once we near London. We'll only feel the tail end of Storm Cleo. That's what they're calling the new storm. As long as the roads stay open, we should get to London in around four hours' time, ETA 5am. Well before any restrictions apply.

I relax my grip on the wheel. I'm back on track, back in control. I understand it all now. Why they were necessary; the guard, Mum, the driver. And now I've demonstrated my loyalty, my commitment, and I know what I need to do, and that I can do it.

'It will be done.'

'What will?' Fee asks.

'Music. What channel do you want? Nighttime groove or party-time pop picks?'

'You're fucking mental.'

'Nighttime groove then.'

I like that her sassiness has come back. I turn around to look at her, give her a smile and when I look back at the road, a dog flies out from the nearside verge about ten yards away. I lift my foot off the accelerator and it makes it across to the other side, but a car approaches from the other direction and for some reason the dog doubles back, cuts right in front of it. I brace myself for the other car to hit the dog, or me, or both of us. Neither happens. The dog manages to squeeze itself out the way but then ends up right in my path. Fee screams as the dog manages another escape, makes it back into the same spot it flew out of.

'Keep your eyes on the road or you'll kill us both.'

I tell her I've no intention of killing any of us. We drive on in silence. Tiredness, exhaustion, they come in useful sometimes.

The roads near the low-lying hills are awash. I have to drive extra slow through the deep water and pump the brakes dry afterwards. We pass an abandoned car half-cock in a ditch, no sign of any police or emergency vehicles. There are fallen branches, and a few fallen trees, but less fallout than I expected.

Monday, 20th June 2022

We reach the M4 as the two o'clock news comes on. Storm Cleo has arrived, and it isn't behaving itself. Wreaking havoc in Wales and Merseyside. Thousands evacuated. The Mersey has burst its banks and a ferry has gone down in the Irish Sea. Storm Cleo was supposed to hug the west coast of Ireland, burn itself out somewhere north west of Scotland, but it didn't. Because there are no rules. Not anymore.

The news ends on a positive note. A young Geordie lass delivers it. 'By dawn Storm Cleo will be well and truly gone, and calm will once again be restored. So, we'll all be able to wake up to blue skies and enjoy our breakfast in peace. I don't know about you lot but I'm having bacon butties.'

'You've forgotten the punchline,' I tell her. 'The bit about the sun making a comeback, the bit about it pouring scorn down upon us. You might want to tell your listeners to make tomorrow's breakfast a good one, because it'll probably be their last.'

My ringtone interrupts. My phone's lying where I left it, on the passenger seat. I look across.

It's Dad's number. I recognise it from Mum's phone. I don't answer it, but he won't stop. I reach over and pick it up. Always wondered what it would be like if I saw him or heard his voice again, because just thinking about him can twist me up in knots.

His voice hasn't changed at all, he sounds exactly the same. But I've changed. I'm not the same.

'Sorry to ring so late,' he says, like he speaks to me every day. Like eight years haven't passed. Like nothing's fucking happened. 'Only I've been trying to get hold of your Mum, but she's not answering.'

I was OK until he mentioned Mum. I pull over on the hard shoulder.

'I rang Celine in the end. The thing is, Celine thinks your mother's visiting me, says you told her that.'

I get out the car and lock the doors. Fee stares at me through the window and I walk to the front of the car. The rain hasn't cooled the air one bit, just made it clammy, muggy.

'She must have got the wrong end of the stick,' I say. 'Celine's always doing that, you know what she's like.'

He knows fuck-all about Celine and he's not happy. He lets out a whistle through his teeth. That was always a dead giveaway, you knew you'd annoyed him when he did that.

'Celine's on a sleepover,' I say. 'She'll have been drinking, probably had a bit of a smoke too. She's got mixed up, that's all. Mum's at home waiting for you but her phone's been playing up, must have finally given out.'

He's chewing gum, can hear his teeth smacking together.

'Can you go wake her up, I need to speak to her.'

A lorry flies past on the inside lane, sprays me with lukewarm water. I tell him I can't, say I'm not at home, that I'm on a sleepover too.

'I can give her a message if you want, in the morning.'

He'll be finding it so hard having to rely on me doing him a favour. He's usually the one in control, usually the one giving the orders. He pauses but he's got no choice.

'You can tell her I'm getting the six o'clock train Tuesday morning. It gets into Kings Cross at half eight, so I should be at the house by half nine.'

'You coming down for the solstice as well as Celine's birthday? Or are you coming down because Mum told you I was setting fires again?'

He will be gripping his phone, screwing up his flinty eyes, trying to sift through every word, trying to work out the fact from the fiction.

'This is what's going to happen,' I tell him. 'You're going to get an earlier train and me and you, we're going to meet up before you go to the house.'

'I'll see you at the house, Luke. I think it's best we stick to the arrangements.'

'You meet me, and I'll hand myself in,' I say. 'You can get to play the big hero and march me off to the cop shop yourself.'

It'll be killing him that I can equal any move he cares to pull. And it's all down to him. He's been such a good teacher. I've learnt from the very best.

'Fine. Where do you want to meet,' he says.

I give him the address of the garage and tell him to go straight there. 'There's a train that gets in for half seven, should give us plenty of time for a catch up.'

'You better show up. This better not be one of your tricks, you better not be leading me a merry dance.'

'I wouldn't do that, Dad,' I say. 'Not on such a special day.'

When we come off the M4 dawn is doing its best to break. 4am and the sun is already powering through, burning up the remaining clouds. Soon every drop of moisture will be gone. Fields that looked like lakes will turn dry as sand, rivers that burst their banks, not so much as a trickle. This is how it will be. Water will evaporate in seconds right before our eyes and people will die. Old people, young people, they'll go first. Those that survive the heat will kill each other out of mercy.

I tune into some other news channels. There's no more talk of the warehouse fire or the dead guard but when they're onto something that's when they go quiet, tread silently. Like a cat, just before the kill.

The petrol indicator has dropped into the reserve area. Can't risk pulling up at a garage with Fee in the car, just got to hope it's a big reserve. I pick up the A40 and then the A46. There's evidence of damage even here, bits of wreckage blow about the North Circ. Litter is strewn across the road and I have to dodge an overturned bin which is on its side in the middle lane. There's hardly any traffic. The roads and streets are almost deserted. People have decided to stay put, not even wait for the restrictions to take place, for the curfew to fall.

At Swiss Cottage the giant displays that blare out the latest must-haves are all streaming the same thing.

SOLAR ACTIVITY EXTREMELY DANGEROUS

CURFEW STAGE 3 IN PLACE

'It's not the storm that's the problem now,' I say. 'Tomorrow the sun will step forward and unleash its fury and you'll see. You'll see why I had to do those things and why I need to do more.'

It's the middle of the night and London's still buzzing with cars, buses, people. This is how it would be if the sun went out. Things wouldn't stop, the capital wouldn't shut down, it would keep on going. We'd keep the lights on, turn the heating up and carry on. I'd want to be in a city though. Wouldn't want to spend a forever night in the sticks. Because it would get to you after a while, no matter where you lived. No matter how much artificial lighting they could use, it would send you mad and your bones would turn to salt. No one could last that long without light. The dark would win in the end.

Alert warnings are everywhere. Every cinema display, every digital ad board, traffic sign, they're all showing the same message. All spelt out in the same burning red pixels. There's nothing displaying the truth though.

'When fire rises in the sky, Earth will reap the wrath, and come the day of reckoning, there will come a saviour.'

'Listen to yourself, you're scaring me, Luke. You're talking like a mad man.'

'It's them you should fear, the deceivers. Still putting out the same old lies, still saying the sun is the enemy, and us, we are the innocent bystanders. No need to fear me, I'm here to protect you. Protect everyone.'

I pass by the road leading to Fee's. She tells me I've missed the turning, but I can take the next one. I carry on.

'I said take the next left.'

'I need to get you to a safe place.'

'I want to go home, take me home.'

The lights are with me, stay green all the way to the very last set. The road running up the west side of the Heath is like a war zone. I'm able to navigate the bigger branches, drive over the smaller ones, but further up a fallen tree has completely blocked our way. I pull over and take my rucksack out the boot, open the passenger door.

She won't look at me, sits with her head hanging forward and her hair covering her face. I take out a torch and a piece of rope from the rucksack.

'I'm going to tie us together and we're going to walk through the Heath. We'll head for the clearing. The trees will provide shade and their leaves will help cool the air.'

I tie the rope around my own wrist and then Fee's. She's doesn't resist. Her wrists are small as a bird, I tell her she's got sparrow bones, toothpick bones. She asks what time it is.

'Daybreak, dawn.'

'I asked for the time.'

'Nearly five o'clock.'

It's getting light but I switch on the torch and tell Fee to stay close by.

'You going to kill me, is that why we're here?'

I tug on the rope and Fee follows. We walk along the narrow path that leads into the Heath. We walk for a good half an hour through a wooded area and what strikes me straight away is how silent it is. No signs or sounds, apart from us.

'How you going to find the clearing at night, wouldn't it have been better to stay put in the car until it got light?'

I know her tricks. If we stay in the car we'll be more visible, more findable. I walk quicker, and tell Fee to keep up. She moans about being thirsty. I tell her when we reach the common I'll give her a drink.

'We're nearly at the common now, clearing's not far from there.'

The wood opens out onto a patch of coarse grassland. In daylight I'd cut across, walk through the tall grass looking for carcasses, carrion, and I'd lay offerings down. I don't want to miss the gap that leads to the clearing, so I lead Fee around the perimeter. Fee wants a toilet break. Tells me to turn away and not look. It's a struggle as her hands are tied but she won't let me help.

When we set off again Fee soon lags behind, drags on the rope. Then stops. She tells me she can't go any further and sinks to her knees. The rope pulls me back and I see she's exhausted.

I take out a tube of soft white mints I got from the glove compartment of the car.

'They'll give you a bit of energy,' I say. 'You can have the lot but don't eat them all at once, it's the only food we've got.'

We cut through to a small copse, the clearing is on the other side.

It's a total car crash. The tepee isn't standing. It's been completely dismantled.

I kick one of the slim silver trunks. All ten of them lie scattered on the ground. I decide the far corner of the clearing would be best to camp down.

'If we rest against this ash tree we'll be sheltered from the sun.'

Fee slumps to the ground and leans her back against the tree. I tell her to take a drink and she asks how much water we have left.

I let her take a few sips and then tell her to raise her arms above her head and cut the rope, keeping her hands bound but freeing the length of it. I use this to bind her to the tree.

'You'll be too hot in your clothes, do you want me to cut your top away?'

She's so weary all she can do is shake her head.

'You should try and get some sleep,' I say.

'How can I? I'm tied to a tree with a rope around my wrists, which you've tied far too tight, it's making my skin sore. Could you loosen it please?'

I use my rucksack as a pillow, hear her sobbing as I close my eyes. Want to tell her it'll soon be over, soon be done, but the tiredness won't let me. I have to let it take me, have to give in to what I know is coming.

The sun won't set. Stays in the sky all day and all night. It's non-stop light and non-stop heat and everyone loves that the sun doesn't go out, doesn't go away. I'm with Fee, we're together, walking in this foggy yellow light. It thickens, becomes more yellow, as the heat builds. Gets so thick I lose sight of her. I keep looking for her, keep bumping into people, thinking it's her but it's not. And then I see her. Fee walks out of the fog towards me. Her belly has grown so big she can hardly walk.

I tell her to lie down because the baby needs to come and I'm scared because she's sweating so much and the air is so thick she can't breathe. I touch her belly and her skin is burning. She wants me to make the heat go away, wants me to make the sun go away but I can't. She pushes and pushes but it won't come. I plead with the sun, beg it to let that baby come, say I'll do anything.

When I wake, I check my phone and see I've slept twelve hours non-stop. Fee is still asleep. I leave her, go searching for food. I don't have to go too far, soon come across wild mushrooms and wild garlic. I manage to gather a handful of each before her screams stop me. She screams for help, for Tilly, for anyone. She screams so loud she flushes a bird out of hiding.

I have to slap her to make her stop. She calms down and I wipe her cheeks, show her the food. She doesn't want any. All she'll have are the mints. I say they're all stuck together but she still won't eat any of the food.

196

'Thought you'd gone, thought you'd left me to die,' she says.

I eat a mushroom. The heat has brought out the flavour. I tell her they taste good, but she's not interested.

The Heath is good at giving shade but it's also good at trapping heat, and as the night falls the warmth becomes suffocating. Fee wants water. I let her have a few sips but no more.

'Are you going to kill me, is that the plan? Is that why you took me to the lighthouse, were you going to do it there?'

'Stop talking, you need to conserve your energy.'

'Have you thought of any names for the baby?'

I shake my head.

'I like short names. That's what's so good about ours. Fee, Luke, they're about as short as you can get. I was thinking Thea for a girl. It means goddess. Haven't thought of any boy's names though.'

I don't want to think about names, think about it being a boy or a girl. I don't want to think about it being, full stop.

'Talk to me, Luke. Tell me something. If this is my last night, I don't want to spend it feeling alone.'

I get up, stretch.

'Any idea how much I've already sacrificed?' I say. 'And it's still not enough. It never is, no matter what I do.

'When we were kids we used to play in this empty house. That's where I carried out my first test, where I first used the sun to set light to something. Even remember what it was, it was an old receipt, a screwed-up bit of paper. I wore specs then, NHS prescription and I used the lens to focus the rays. Celine used to watch me, and one time she stole my specs and went back there on her own, but she put the paper on top of an old mattress and the mattress caught alight and the house burnt down. There was a homeless guy asleep upstairs and he nearly died. They found my specs and I got blamed and I took the blame because I felt guilty. She was my kid sister, and I should have known better. She was only copying me, that's what kids do.'

'It was an accident, Luke, it was no one's fault.'

'It's OK, it was all preparation. I saved her and now look what I'm about to do. I'm about to save the fucking world.'

I stand in the middle of the clearing, ask for guidance one final time.

Send me your strength.

Show me what I need to do.

197

Tuesday, 21st June 2022

I don't sleep, doze on and off. Fee snores all night because her breathing's restricted from her head falling forward. The sun I wake up to is not a pale or weak sun. It's a strong, bright sun.

I dig at the dry ground with my knife. Carve out a shape as best as I can. I tell Fee I won't be long but that the Sun God will protect her.

She asks for water and I bend down to give her some and she spits in my face. I go to wipe her mouth and she sinks her teeth into my finger. I slam my other hand into her forehead, push her head back against the tree and she lets go with her teeth. There's a technique, where you lean in real close to the enemy's face and hit them with your voice. Scream orders, questions, anything you can think of, for as long as you can.

'You need to listen to me. This is the day we pay our respects, the day we perform our duties. If we don't, punishment will follow, and it will be deserved. I can stop this. I can free us. You, me, everyone.'

'You've tied me to a tree like a prisoner, I'm pregnant, with your baby and now you're going to abandon me, leave me here to die. Please, Luke, you're not thinking straight. You're talking like a madman. Cut me free, Luke, please'

'It's too late, it's already begun. Can't you see.'

I point upwards, at the light falling through the trees.

'You tied the rope too tight. It's hurting me, it's digging into my belly, it's hurting the baby. Please loosen it, I promise I won't run away.'

She cries out and draws her knees up to her chin.

'I might lose the baby, Luke. Whatever I've done, please don't punish the baby, it's done nothing!'

She lets out a high-pitched sound. It's the noise a pig might make having its throat cut. The final sound that stains the slayer, points the finger.

I take out my knife, slide a cutting blade free. Slip it between rope and skin. Slices clean, easy. Fee wriggles her hands free and then tugs at the rope binding her to the tree. She kicks the cut rope away as she scrambles to her feet. We stand there looking at each other, less than two yards separate us.

I throw her a bottle of water. She catches it and we stand watching each other, the way cats do. She turns and runs, doesn't stop. I hear her smash her way through the bushes, hear things snap under feet. I won't go until I hear the very last sound she makes.

When I exit the Heath, the car is still parked up by the roadside. They'll have filed a report by now, but they'll put it down to the storm, think the car's ended up in a ditch somewhere. As long as it buys me a few more hours, that's all I need.

I turn left at the mini-roundabout into the road that leads to Childs' Hill. All the rain that fell has been burnt away, and the strength of the sun is melting the road. The tarmac is sticky, spongy. I step onto the pavement. The stone slabs are coping a lot better. Further on, I pass a dog lying in the middle of the road. Eyes bulging, tongue swollen. Not been dead long. Looks like a Border cross. A dog built for running around fields, built for working, herding sheep in rain and snow and now it's lying on a molten road with blackened paws.

I wipe the sweat from my face and grab a cold can from the ice stand. The patrols have been busy. It's something at least. As I grab another can a solar patrol flies past, it pulls over ahead of me. I cross to the opposite side and drink as I walk. It's not me they're interested in. They've stopped a woman with an old pram. It looks like she's pushing her whole life around in it. They want to take her away, for her own safety. Dad used to say that to me, in the same voice. The one that made him sound like he cared, and then he'd introduce my worst fear. Show it off like it was his best fucking friend. Now you see it. Now you don't. Now you see it. Now you don't.

I stick to the shade, walk as close to the buildings as I can. It's only a three mile walk but I've already sweated through every layer of clothing and my face is pouring with water, like I've stepped straight out of the pool. Sweat's the body's natural coolant but ice from the stand works better. I grab a handful of cubes and drop them down the front of my t-shirt. They're already melting and it's not even 7am. Dad's train will be arriving in forty minutes. I check Mum's phone. There's a text from earlier. *ON TRAIN. BE THERE SOON.* I text back OK.

Everything's closed, the streets are empty. The curfew hasn't officially started yet but the streets have emptied and all the shops are closed because the only safe place to be is inside. There's a water stand outside Willesden tube but it's already struggling, the ice has turned to slush and the stand has filled with water. I stick my hands inside, keep them there for a few seconds, let my wrists cool down.

As I turn right at the mini-roundabout I see someone a few yards up from the garage. It's Scarlet. No mistaking that hair and no mistaking the car she's hurrying towards. Malik's silver Mini is parked up and soon as she gets into it, it speeds away before I get the chance to check if anyone's with her.

I walk on, stand outside the door, read the sign.
WE ARE CLOSED UNTIL FURTHER NOTICE.
APOLOGIES TO ALL OUR CUSTOMERS
Malik was right, Kojak's past has caught up with him. Today is the day of reckoning for all of us. I'm about to step up and give the performance of my life and I've never felt so ready, so focused. It's not all about logic, planning. At the final act, theatre has a part. It's where everything comes together, where all the energy centres and where all the preparation will carry you through.

I turn the key in the lock, open the door. The bell jingles as I step inside and I get ready for the alarm to sound but it doesn't. There's only quiet, stillness. I close the door behind me and walk through reception. Soon as I step into the back room I smell it. Soon as I look through the window I see him. Malik's in the yard, waving a petrol cannister about, emptying the contents all over the cars.

He's got his back to me and when I open the back door, he swings around so fast he nearly falls over.

'What you doing?' I ask.

'What I should have done weeks ago. What's it to you, anyway? And why are you here? Aren't you supposed to be on the run? Or did you run out of money already? Fancied dropping by, did you, seeing if you can rob some more, while Kojak's otherwise engaged? Got to give it you, you got some balls.' The sound of a siren shuts him up. He throws the cannister to the floor. 'That's not heading our way,' he says.

I put my hands in my pocket, wrap my fingers around the warm metal.

'Whoa!'

He takes a step back when he sees the knife in my hand. I flick the locking blade and he backs away even further. 'No need for tools, man. No need for that.'

I jab the blade at him and he runs towards the back gates and scrambles over them. Hear his feet pound the pavement, hear the sirens get nearer. It doesn't leave me, that sense of certainty stays put. The sirens fade and I realise I should have thanked Malik for his help. He's done good. All I need to do is set up the mirrors, and as I position the last one can feel the heat is already itching to bring the fumes alive.

There are two cars in the work bays, a smart car and a hybrid. I check my phone, no messages, no missed calls. Dad should be here by now, if he's still coming. If he hasn't called in to the house first, found Mum, rung the police.

I lay it down on the bonnet of the smart car and have a look around. The workshop's a mess. Tools everywhere. Can tell Mo's not been around, he always kept things neat and tidy.

As I walk towards the other car I hear footsteps, they're quick, fleeting. Something strikes the back of my legs and I sprawl across the bonnet of the hybrid. As I try to get up, I get hit again and slide to the floor. I look up, see Dad standing over me, front end of an exhaust pipe in his fist. He bends down and shoves the pipe under my chin. The sight of him, threatening me with a stick of metal, makes me want to laugh.

'Think you're so clever, don't you?' he says. His eyes have got puffy and his face is lined but he still looks exactly the same. 'Think it's funny setting fires, destroying property, destroying people?'

I can't hold it in. I have to laugh out loud, have to laugh right in his face. He lifts the pipe in the air, goes to hit me with it but I roll away soon as he lifts his arm, soon as he shifts his weight. I grab a wrench from the ledge by the back wall and duck down behind the smart car.

'You'd know all about destroying people,' I say.

Dad edges towards me and I tell him not to come any closer. There's an air pressure gun next to my foot, the tubing coiled beneath it like a snake.

'I've got a gun,' I shout.

He makes that sigh, the one he always made when I'd try to bluff my way out of harm. 'The police will be here any minute,' he says. 'Be a whole lot better if you'd be a man about this, do the right thing.'

What does he know about being a man, doing the right thing?

'Me, Mum and Celine, we were doing fine without you. Why couldn't you leave us alone? Why have you got to turn up now? You want to play the big hero, you want to be the one to take me in? Think it will impress Mum, is that it?

'I'm going to tell you something that I was going to save for your first prison visit. Until you came along, me and your Mum, we were doing fine. Soon as you hit the deck everything changed, it was all Luke this, Luke that. She thought the sun shone out of you. I told her it wouldn't last, told her you'd turn out a bad-un, and I was right, wasn't I?'

He carries on and I let him. While he's rambling he's not paying attention. I crouch down, look underneath the smart car. I see past his boots, to the cars behind him, to the pools of petrol swimming between them.

'Just the other week, your Mum was telling me you'd changed, got yourself a job. What went wrong?'

He stands looking at his phone, as if he's waiting for a bus, acting like Mr Fucking Cool. He's got the same black trousers on and white shirt he always wore. The same bull neck, the same creeping hairline.

'Come on out, your mother will be waiting for us.'

'Don't you mean the police. Isn't that who you've been ringing?'

He sighs and puts the phone in his pocket. 'Don't make me come and get you, son.'

'You can't tell me what to do anymore. You can't make me do what you want.'

The sun intensifies on the mirror and the petrol catches. I can see small wings of flames dancing on the ground behind him.

'Suit you down to the ground, me banged up, wouldn't it!' I say.

'Should've happened years ago. I'd still have a wife and I'd still have a daughter. Never mind, all good things come to those who wait, isn't that what they say?'

'Sorry to disappoint, but Mum's gone and she's never coming back.'

Our eyes lock and there's a spasm, deep down in my belly. It rolls on up through my chest, pushes against my ribs. Keeps pushing.

A noise like something from a sci-fi movie rips out of me. It knocks him backwards and he stumbles over something on the floor, something not put away, something left lying around. I walk towards him and all he can do is retreat. He backs out of the workshop into the yard. Stands in front of the car. A band of yellow light flickers underneath it. The flames have spread, grown stronger.

Dad takes his phone out, tries to make a call, but he can't because his fingers won't do what he wants them to.

'It's fear, Dad,' I say. 'That's what it does. It makes you fuck up the simplest of tasks. Do you remember my fear? My fear of the dark? Do remember what you did? To make me feel better, less afraid. You used to switch my light off, leave me lying the dark, crying myself to sleep, sometimes I'd wet the bed, wouldn't I, and that would make you angry and so you'd tell me a little bedtime story. What was it you used to say?'

He gives up with his phone, looks at me as if he wants me to repeat the question.

'I've remembered,' I tell him. 'You used to tell me the sun could go out just as easy, that was it. And then you'd show me, wouldn't you? You'd switch the light on and off. Now you see it, now you don't. And you'd tell your mates down the pub, you'd think it was funny me lying in the pitch dark, not being able to sleep because I was scared, scared the sun had gone out. Scared it had gone and left me. Left me in the dark forever.'

'I can smell petrol,' he says to me. 'Smelt it when I came, one of the cars must be leaking.'

'You're not *listening*,' I shout. 'That's rude. I was talking about the little game you used to play. Now you see me, now you don't. I haven't brought you here for that, though. I'm happy to forget the past, because what you did brought us closer. Me and the sun, we're one. I know everything about that burning star in the sky and it knows everything about me. Did you know it's four and a half billion years old, Dad? Got a core temperature of fifteen million degrees centigrade. I know a lot more, and that's because of you. I want to thank you. You gave me my destiny.'

The smell of burning rubber hits the back of my throat. Dad can smell it too. He looks around, tries to work out where it's coming from and when he does he points as if I don't know the car's on fire. He backs away, walks across the yard, yells for me to come out the workshop. He's back to giving me orders and fully expecting me to obey.

'Where's your extinguisher, your fire blanket?'

He's panicking. I realise I've never seen him panic before. He's on to the emergency services, telling them about the fire, when the first car explodes. We both try and dodge the broken glass, the bits of shorn metal. The car's roof has been ripped off, the windows shattered and the interior filled with flames. A second later another car goes up, and then another. Fireworks timed to perfection.

Thick smoke billows up and I stand inside a cloud of black snow. Shrapnel glinting as it swirls about me. The blast deafened me and it's so peaceful, so quiet. The charred pieces twist and turn graceful as acrobats, up and up they go, sucked towards the giant fireball rising above the garage.

I walk towards the cars, now completely consumed by a wall of flames. It's like the TV footage they kept showing. The sheets of red and yellow, the cackling spitting sound as they tore through the warehouse. This time I'm not watching from a distance, I'm not rewinding the scene over and over, this time I'm here. Witnessing for myself.

This is how I imagine it, the surface of the sun. The hissing rage, the spitting fury. The glory of it all. I move towards it but Dad has me by my wrist. His thick fingers dig into my skin as he tries to pull me away. His arm is at full stretch, his other is up protecting his face. I don't go any closer and he relaxes his grip.

Everything has led to this. This day of punishment and revenge, forgiveness and redemption. Our pain, and our past, has brought us here. Only we can do this, only we can ensure a future.

A curl of flame breaks free. *Come in.*

In the end it's easy.

Just like the driver, all it takes is one quick pull. I hug him, for the first time. I tell him I forgive him. Then I close my eyes. The heat, sharp as blades, cuts into me. He screams as we fall, but I don't hear him above the noise of the fire. *We've been waiting*, it roars, *we've been waiting.*

So have I, I say. So have I.

Epilogue

August, 2024

You could still smell it when we moved in, could still taste it. I said we should wait a few weeks because it might be bad for Thea. It's only paint, Fee said, but I was right. Thea started with a bad cough straight away, took weeks to go.

The Services didn't just redecorate, they took things. My laptop, iPad, Mum's old phones. The shed. They actually got a JCB in. Picked it up and took it away in one piece. And they spent weeks stripping Luke's room, took it right back to the plasterwork. Light switches, curtain poles, the lot. They said it was to help with the investigation but that was two years and they still haven't given any of the stuff back. They've still got Mum's body. Keep saying they'll organise a ceremony, so we can say our goodbyes, but they never do.

I tell Emilia this, but she's more interested in a feel-good storyline, wants to focus on our uber family set up.

'They've no right to keep hold of Mum all this time,' I say.

I have to speak quite loud because Emilia's office is noisy but I don't want to wake Thea. She's asleep next door, but she wakes so easily. Emilia asks me how the shared care is going. I say fine and then she asks about Fee.

'You will mention they've still got Mum's body, won't you? They shouldn't be allowed to do that.'

Emilia promises me she will. She's got kind eyes and I like her hair. If mine was bang straight, I'd have my fringe cut all sharp and jaggy like shark's teeth. Emilia doesn't seem sharp and jaggy but the case worker from The Services said people aren't always what they seem.

Someone else is having a conversation next to Emilia and they're really loud. Emilia apologises and pushes her face closer to the screen and I do the same.

'What you said about the money, it will go straight into my account, right?' I ask.

'Once the article has been published on the website.'

'What if it isn't published?'

'I have no doubt the story will get published, Celine, it's exactly the kind of thing our readers want. Excuse me, can you give me a second.'

Emilia moves away from the screen and I get to see more of the office. Two men are standing behind her, backs to me, both of them working at the same giant screen. It's huge, runs right along the back wall.

'Shall we do a quick recap and then we can crack on,' Emilia says when she comes back into view. She fires it all back to me and when she's finished she drops her head to the side. 'You've been so brave, Celine, you lost your family in such tragic circumstances. Your brother was obviously a very troubled young man. Can I ask if he'd shown any signs that might suggest he could do something like this?'

'You mean, did I know he was psycho? Did I know he'd end up killing both my parents and himself?'

'I wouldn't put it quite like that.'

'"Madness and genius go hand and hand. They said Galileo was mad because he believed the earth was round when everyone else believed it was flat. But it turned out he was the sane one."'

She swivels her eyes right, signals something to the person sitting next to her.

'Oh, they're not my words, they're Fee's. She's the clever one, she's a maths whizz. Luke was good at numbers but she's better. She thinks he could have made a mistake, got the date wrong, she's doing her own research.'

Emilia looks down at her notes, then back at me.

'Shall we call it a day, Celine? I can write up what I've got and if you think of anything else, you can email me. Let's just keep it about the three of you for now. You, Fee, Thea. I think your story of survival and hope is going to go down really well. Oh, and if you have any recent pictures, of you, Fee and Thea, that would be good.'

Emilia gives me a quick wave then the screen goes black. I tell my computer to sleep and go into Fee's room.

She's kneeling at the wall, black marker pen in hand, printouts scattered around her.

'They're going with it,' I say. 'And they're going to pay.'

Fee shushes me. 'Don't wake Thea, she's just gone down.'

I sit on the edge of Fee's bed, rock the cot beside it. Thea likes to sleep with her arms up by her head. It's her surrender pose. The Services said all babies sleep like that. I look around at Luke's old room. Apart from being newly painted, and Thea's cot, it's pretty much back the same as it was now. Calendars all over the place, back wall covered in sums.

The marker pen squeaks as Fee adds another sum to the wall. Fee needs more printouts. Now. When she shouts her orders like that she makes Thea jump. Makes her eyes pop out, makes her little legs and arms fling wide open. Thea does her unhappy grizzle and I feel it, the sharp tug in my chest, like we're stitched together.

'Can you please go print out the rest of the calendars.'

Thea lets out a cry and I lift her from the cot and cuddle her. She falls against me, soft and floppy and straight away her mouth makes like a fish. Opens and shuts. Opens and shuts. And her head bobs about looking for food. No milk here, baby, I say, and kiss the top of her head. It's warm, too warm. The Services said to give her plenty of water. Said it was very important to keep her well hydrated, especially in the dry season, because babies don't have as good temperature control as grownups. That's why they put in new air conditioning units because the ones we had were old and weren't good enough. And she has to stay inside most of the day until she's four, so they gave us special lamps to sit her in front of. Like her very own suns.

Thea lets out a fart. 'She needs changing,' I say. 'I'll sort the printouts soon as I've given her a new nappy.'

I lay Thea down on the bed, tell her we will have to stop feeding her, if she's going to keep pooing. Thea claps her hands together and pulls a cheeky smile. I take out the baby wipes and the small towel from the basket under the cot. Thea always knows when its clean nappy time. We play a game where she kicks her legs out really fast and I have to grab her ankles. I lift her bum up in the air, slide the towel underneath and take off the loaded nappy. My nappies go on super quick and super easy. The Services said I was a very quick learner.

'You love a clean nappy, don't you,' I say, and Thea lets out a squeal.

'I need those printouts,' Fee says.

I lean in, pull a face at Thea and she squeals again. Fee doesn't even notice. She's never happier than when she's scribbling all over the wall. Luke was the same.

'Why you doing this? It didn't happen, the sun is still here. It didn't go out, it didn't die.'

'It's good to keep an open mind and it's good to check all evidence. I know the sun's still here but look at how we exist. Children under four not allowed out of the house for half the year, houses fitted with blackouts and day lights, people suffocating going to work. It's becoming the norm and it's not. It is so far away from being normal.'

'Why don't I take Thea out? It's gone five now. You can get on with what you need to do. Be back in an hour and then I can make dinner.'

Fee nods and I dress Thea in her favourite all-in-one. She likes the bright colours, claps her hands every time she wears it.

'Say bye to Mummy,' I say.

Downstairs I fasten Thea into her pushchair, brush her hair out of her eyes before I put on her hat. Sometimes, when we're out, people think I'm her Mum because we've got the same dark brown hair. I don't say anything. I let them think I am.

Acknowledgments

Thanks to everyone at Mayfly Press and New Writing North, especially Claire Malcolm for her continued belief and support. Thanks to Pauline, Linda, Kate, Pat, Lesley, Michelle, Tricia, Bernard, Guy, Joe, Lara, Freya, Georgia, Val, Pam, Christina, Kay, John, Lee, Angela, Rachel, Chizu, Lynne, Trudi, Virginia, Karen, Sarah, Helen. Biggest thanks to Bernie and Lib, I owe you so much.

Thanks to Willesden Green Writing Group, Sheffield MA writing group, Broomspring Writers, Hallam Writers, Arts Council England, TLC Free Reads, Arvon Grants, WEA. Thanks to the NHS, to UCLH, The Royal Marsden, St Marks, James Cook University Hospital. To Macmillan Cancer Support, Lynch Syndrome UK.

Lastly, love and thanks to my roots, to the Browns and the Bashfords, to all the buds and all the branches. May the warmth, the laughter, never die.

About the author

Jude Brown grew up in Middlesbrough and has lived in London, Liverpool, Reading and Sydney. She has had a varied career to date, including working as a medical secretary, nurse, designer, art therapist and writing tutor. She moved to Sheffield for an MA in Creative Writing at Sheffield Hallam University, where she began writing *His Dark Sun*, her first novel. Her short stories and poems have been published in several anthologies and her work has been shortlisted for the Bridport and Raymond Carver Short Story Prizes. She is the recipient of a Northern Writers' Award and the writing of *His Dark Sun* was supported by a grant from Arts Council England.

@joodebrown
www.judebrown.co.uk